LOTTY DISHES THE DIRT

Diane Ezzard

Other Books in the Series: -

Dotty Dices with Death – Book 1

Dotty Dreads a Disaster – Book 2 (Coming soon)

Other books by Diane Ezzard

The Sophie Brown mystery series –

> My Dark Decline – prequel to the series.

1. I Know Your Every Move
2. As Sick As Our Secrets
3. The Sinister Gathering
4. Resentments and Revenge
5. A Life Lost
6. The Killing Cult

Website: http://dezzardwriter.com/
Email: support@dezzardwriter.com
Facebook: https://www.facebook.com/dezzardwriter/
Twitter: https://twitter.com/diane_ezzard

Newsletter Sign-up

I hope you enjoy reading my novella as much as I enjoyed writing it. I am looking to build a relationship up with my readers, so occasionally I will be sending out newsletters. These will include otherwise untold information about the characters, things about myself, and other bits of news.

I would love you to join us and in return for giving me your email which will never be passed on to third parties, you will receive exciting offers and give-aways not found anywhere else.

You can find the sign-up page on my website at:

http://dezzardwriter.com/mc4wp-form-preview

TABLE OF CONTENTS

Other books by the author	2
Newsletter Sign up	3
Table of contents	4
Novel	5
Newsletter sign up reminder	120
Review request	121
About the Author	122
Acknowledgements	123
Blurbs and extracts	124
Full Bibliography	141

Chapter 1

"Nothing exciting ever happens here." Dotty gazed up at the skylight and followed the ray of sun shining down on top of her slice of cake. The dusting of icing sugar glistened. Kylie glanced at the people sat at the other tables and nodded.

"If this is the place to come to see some action, then the over-sixties crowd sat in the corner should put their crosswords away and take up skydiving." A family who turned up for a birthday celebration sat devouring a variety of cakes. She agreed that life in the village of Billingshurst could be boring.

"It's all happening here. A cat got stuck up a tree last week and the fire brigade got called." Kylie eyed up the row of cakes on display in the glass cabinet as she sunk her teeth into the coffee and walnut cake in her hand. Eating with a fork was too dainty for her.

"Exactly. Do you wish you had a more interesting job?"

"No, pulling pints is exciting enough for me."

"Do you regret not going to university?" Dotty asked. A splodge of fresh cream oozed out from her Victoria sponge cake, and she scooped it up with her elegant gel-manicured pinkie. She closed her eyes and swooned with delight at the orgasmic taste. As she deposited the remaining portion back on the plate, a bite mark of red lipstick glowed on the rest of the slice. Dotty didn't go anywhere without wearing her bright pillar-box red lipstick and she freshened up at every opportunity.

"Nah, I thought it best to leave my place to someone with brains," Kylie replied. She watched as Dotty took a sip of her tea. Her little finger was held apart from the rest of her digits as she placed the delicate china cup back on the mismatched saucer.

"You're not that thick."

"Thanks, Dotty. I love you too."

"No seriously, do you ever fancy doing anything other than bar work?"

"At least I've got a job."

Dotty glared at her friend.

"I'm looking. I go online every day to see what's available. It's not easy in this economic climate."

"You can't blame Brexit for you not getting off your lazy butt." Dotty laughed.

"You're right. I could put more effort in." Dotty nodded. "I'm too fond of daytime TV. You know how enthralled I get from watching Homes under the Hammer and Dickenson's Real Deal. What I wouldn't give to find a Ming vase in the attic, hidden underneath last year's Christmas decorations."

"If you're looking for a 'get-rich-quick' scheme, it's not going to happen. You must do some serious grafting if you want to come on holiday next year with me and Rachel." Dotty sighed. She knew her friend was right. She would have to put more effort into looking for employment.

"I can't wait. A fortnight in the sun on a Spanish beach – drinking sangria and having suntan oil rubbed in my back by some Mediterranean hunk." Dotty closed her eyes and drifted off to the Costa del wherever. "I don't mind where we go. My tick list is small — sun, sea and a nice senor. If that isn't possible, then I'd settle for a trip to La Tomatina festival – the world's biggest food fight. Twenty thousand people gather each year near Valencia to throw tomatoes at each other. That sounds fun, doesn't it, Kylie?"

"You wouldn't be happy there. You create a drama if you get a mark on your clothes." Dotty scowled. "Talking of Rachel, where is she? She's late again. If she doesn't hurry up, we'll have finished without her."

Dotty checked the time on her brand-new silver Seksy watch – a recent birthday present from her mum and dad. It was more than she received from her younger brother, Joe. He bought her a tin of soup. Yes, a tin of soup! Well, it was Heinz tomato, her favourite, and he said that it was the thought that counted. Dotty wasn't convinced. He'd probably forgotten her birthday again and called in the corner shop on his way home. The soup was no doubt meant for his evening meal, but he wouldn't own up to Dotty that he had forgotten her birthday. Instead, he described it as a unique present, something she would use. Dotty was not impressed. He didn't even splash out for the family size.

A similar incident happened two years before with the Christmas present that he got her. Dotty had been invited with her mum and dad to spend the festive season with her auntie Jean. Auntie Jean was very wealthy and lived in a six-bedroomed mansion in Dorset. She made her money from shoes. Auntie Jean was an excellent and respected designer who set up her own company and manufactured and sold her shoes all over the world. Dotty's mum, Gloria was her only sister and last remaining relative. When Gloria had a health scare and a mini-heart attack, Auntie Jean worried she would lose her only sister, so the family were invited to stay over the holiday period.

Dotty wished that more of her family would get ill. She loved spending time at Auntie Jean's home. She got to sample Jean's expensive skincare products and dabbed on the skin caviar and other finery. Closing her eyes, she imagined living the luxury lifestyle. Dotty often daydreamed about having a butler or a housekeeper at least.

On Christmas morning, they had gathered in the drawing-room to open their presents. Dotty had sneaked a peek at her presents the previous night. Patience was not one of her virtues. She felt each present, smelt the wrapping paper, shook them and then deduced that her brother Joe must have splashed out and bought her something decent. The square box looked suspiciously like the packaging for her favourite perfume. She couldn't smell any scent, but she was convinced that was what was inside. She was impressed.

When the reveal ceremony took place, Dotty saved Joe's present until last. She had already opened a beautiful cashmere jumper off her auntie and a new hairdryer from her mum and dad. She glanced over at Joe, grinning in anticipation as she tore through the silver reindeer and snowmen.

The box looked like a used perfume container. Dotty frowned. Something wasn't right. She scurried inside, beavering away to open the package. She picked up the jar and held it aloft to gasps from the others.

"Bovril!"

"Yes, you know, it's a great beef flavoured drink for cold winter nights." Joe laughed.

"Bovril, Joe?" Dotty's mum questioned.

"You like a drink of Bovril, don't you, Dotty?" Joe asked.

"I do, but I wasn't expecting to get a jar for Christmas. It's an unusual present, Joe."

"I thought it would be a surprise. I didn't think you'd guess what it was."

"Well, you were right." Dotty shook her head.

"I guessed you'd be sick of getting the same old perfume, so I thought of something different." Dotty sighed. He must have spent all of three pounds on her gift. She wished she hadn't splashed out on that gym bag for him. He noticed the look of shock on her face and tried to appease her.

"It's the thought that counts and I'd much rather you have a gift that won't go to waste," he said."

"Quite," Dotty replied. Her stunned expression rippled around the room amongst the others.

She was too nice to get her own back when it was his birthday. She considered buying him shaving foam. Joe was sixteen at the time and hadn't reached the stubble stage of his development yet. He kept shaving in the hope of a beard appearing overnight.

Her memories of Joe's unusual presents were disturbed as the door to The Strawberry tea rooms swung open and Rachel breezed in. She looked younger than her twenty-seven years with her modern balayage hairstyle with blonde tips. Curls cascaded down her back and most people would be forgiven for thinking she had hair extensions, but Rachel had been blessed with a thick head of hair.

Dotty often felt like the poor relation in Rachel's presence. However, she didn't dress like someone out of work. Today she wore a coral and white polka dot wrap dress. Her gold drop shell design earrings tinkled as she moved her head.

Kylie commented that in the beauty stakes, Rachel had an unfair advantage over her friends. As well as her long golden tresses, she had stunning blue eyes to match the rest of her looks and a body to die for. At five foot ten she towered over the other two. They often told her she could have been a model. Rachel hadn't been confident enough to enter that field and worked instead in an office as an administrator.

Heads turned when Rachel walked in the room, but today it wasn't her stunning good looks that got the friends sitting up in their seats. No, the sight that got them popping their heads around like a couple of meerkats, was the guy who arrived behind her.

"Psst, that's your neighbour, Hans Mueller, isn't it?" Kylie whispered.

"You're right and I don't know who that young woman is that he's with, but it's not his wife."

Chapter 2

The Strawberry tea rooms was the girls' go-to place where they discussed their problems. Even though Dotty was cash-strapped, she couldn't cut down on their weekly visit to the elegant café. With its white walls festooned with pink silk roses and white wisteria, it had just the right amount of grace and style. The grey and white marble tables matched the French period feature chairs. The walls were painted white, and the place was clean and inviting. According to Dotty, it was the sort of establishment where Audrey Hepburn wouldn't have looked out of place.

Rachel sat next to the other two girls thankful that they had something else to focus on rather than her tardiness. She had her story prepared but for now, they were happy to debate who the mystery woman could be.

"Surely, she's too young to be his bit on the side." Kylie nudged Dotty's arm.

"Stop it, Kylie. I can't keep staring. It's best that he doesn't spot I'm here." Dotty had pulled the laminated menu up over her face.

"It'd be great to get something on him if he is up to no good, especially after the trouble he caused over your car."

"That's true. Anyone would think he owned the road. Perhaps it was different when he lived in Germany, but he had no right to put cones out to stop me parking outside his house." Dotty's lips narrowed. "He keeps putting cones there, and I keep moving them. I have a large supply now hidden in our shed. I could set up my own roadworks, I've got that many traffic cones."

"What would your dad say if he saw them?" Rachel asked.

"He wouldn't be too pleased. With his job in the police force, he expects everyone to be saints. He went berserk when I nicked a pencil from school once. If he knew about the cones, he'd have me locked in stocks in the village and get everyone to throw rotten fruit at me. Thinking about it, I should drop the cones off at your flat one night when the coast is clear. Putrid fruit wouldn't do my complexion much good."

Rachel shook her head at the thought.

"What would I do with a load of orange and white cones? I couldn't say they were a feature or turn them upside down and disguise them as vases." The girls laughed.

"Anyway, Rachel," Kylie said. "You're not sneaking in and getting away with being late today without a bloody good excuse."

"I've got one. I had important business to attend to." She wafted the menu in front of her face. Perspiration gathered on her forehead, brought on by the warm sunny day and not because she was worried. The pretty young waitress came and stood over her. "I'll have an Earl Grey tea, thanks, Belinda."

She turned towards her two friends and with a pronounced frown said, "I'm worried about Grandad George."

Kylie and Dotty raised their eyebrows as though they both wondered, "What cock and bull story are you going to string us along with this time?"

Rachel continued, "I was late because I visited my grandad." Rachel pulled a face. "He's gone downhill, ever since Nana Mavis went into a home. I don't know if putting her in there was a good idea."

"But she has dementia. He didn't have any choice." Kylie wrinkled her forehead.

"True, but he's not coping on his own. His eyesight is failing, and he struggles to get around with his bad back and knees. You should see his garden. It's a jungle."

"There you go, Dotty. Why don't you become a gardener?" Kylie punched her friend's arm. "It's not that hard. You could borrow your dad's mower for now. That's all most old people need. There are plenty of them around here who would be glad of a cheery young girl to keep on top of things. You could start with Rachel's grandad's house, just as a trial and see how you like it."

"That's a brilliant idea. What do you think, Dotty?" Rachel asked.

"I don't know. It sounds hard work to me."

"Why not come over and help me sort out Grandad George's garden and take it from there? You'd be doing him a big favour, and you'd find out if you enjoyed it. I mean you like flower arranging, don't you?"

"Yeah, but flowers aren't caked in mud and I don't know my weeds from my wisteria."

"Hmm," Rachel said, stroking her chin, "that could be a problem. Let's go over to my grandad's house. We could turn it into a fun afternoon."

After exhausting the list of the plants and flowers they knew, they moved their attention back to Hans and the mystery woman. The couple had finished their drinks and were making a move. The friends hadn't come up with any legitimate suggestions about why they would be sat together. They looked very intimate and cosy, chatting next to each other. All eyes were on the pair as they left. Dotty's eyebrows were raised, and as they closed the door behind them, she winked at her two friends.

Chapter 3

Dotty arrived at Grandad George's house the following day, along with a hoe, a rake and a spade she'd fished out of her parents' garden shed. Dotty wouldn't admit it, but she didn't have a clue what to do with the equipment. She figured the spade was for digging but that was the sum total of her knowledge.

She had met Grandad George many times in the past. When she first started senior school, she and Rachel would sometimes get picked up by Rachel's grandparents. She always received a handful of chocolate eclairs and a ham sandwich, if she was really hungry. His tiny front garden and average-sized semi didn't give any clues as to what lay at the back. She knew though how big his garden was and what size the job was she had let herself in for.

She gazed across at George and thought how much he had aged since the last time she visited. His deep wrinkles carved out a map on his face — curves and lines that held the secrets of a well-lived past. His once twinkling blue eyes now appeared hollow and weary. When he tried to muster a smile, his yellowing teeth showed. His face had thinned out and looked gaunt. His cheekbones stuck out like a skeleton.

George sat in his upright armchair, the only addition to the furniture in the last thirty years. The sofa was redundant for George now. If he sat on it, he could no longer get up, so he spent his days in his trusted green velour chair. There was even a pocket to place the remote control if George remembered to use it.

"How are you doing, Grandad George?"

"I'm doing alright, my darling. I can't grumble." George could grumble. In fact, he moaned all the time about something. Poor Rachel got the brunt of his negativity as she was the family member who visited him the most.

George still had a strong Cockney accent. He was brought up in the east end of London, the same as his family before him. He started work at Billingsgate market. When he married Mavis, they moved to Sussex, and he worked in a local fish and chip shop. Some years later, he got a job as a chef in a country pub and did that until he retired. Back in those days, you didn't need qualifications, but George had always enjoyed cooking so preferred to take charge in the kitchen. In their early married life, it was frowned upon for the man to do the cooking. However, George liked to think of himself as a modern man, something of a pioneer. He didn't feel very modern anymore though with his aches and pains and constant visits to the hospital over one thing or another.

"Dotty has come to do your garden, Grandad George." Rachel smiled at Dotty. Her reaction was to pull the sides of her mouth in a downwards fashion, the way a lizard might.

"That's very kind of you, dear. I haven't done any gardening for a while, with my bad back. It's a jungle out there. I've let it go." To say it was a jungle was an understatement. George could sell tickets and promote the garden as a maze, or a wildlife park and he would still be within the Trades Description Act. A few minutes trampling in the overgrown area, and you'd soon get lost. You might even encounter a wild animal if you were lucky. Foxes, rabbits and squirrels were common sightings, poking their heads out of the tall grass.

Dotty had brought her poodle along for moral support and because Grandad George liked Winnie. George thought more of Winnie than he did most humans. When Winnie was there, she became his main focus.

"I have some dog biscuits in the cupboard if you can fetch them in, Rachel. I bought them especially for Winnie the poodle, didn't I, girl?" George said as he ruffled up the dog's curly mop of hair. Winnie's tail wagged.

There was a knock at the front door. Dotty answered. Rachel was busy in the kitchen making a cup of tea. Dotty spotted the outline straightaway. The ample bosom and solid frame topped with bleached platinum hair with a lilac streak in the front could mean only one thing — Kylie had decided to join them.

"I thought I'd come along and give you some support. I know a thing or two about plants. My family think I'm not just green-fingered but green-toed as well."

"Yuck, sounds repulsive." Dotty stood aside as her friend marched down the hall. "Rachel's put the kettle on. Nip through to the kitchen."

The girls spent twenty minutes sipping their tea and chatting with George. George was a war baby, born the day that Britain declared war on Germany. Whilst the rest of the family were gathered around the wireless listening to Neville Chamberlain's speech, George's mum was upstairs giving birth to a bouncing baby boy.

George often liked to recount his early memories, especially his earliest one. He recalled Winston Churchill's speech declaring the end of the war in 1945 and everyone going out into the streets cheering and partying. He reminisced about food rationing and the British bulldog spirit. These days he had lost that rallying spirit and only moved from his armchair to visit his wife.

The girls loved listening to his stories, but there was work to be done. They needed to act sharpish if they were to make a start before the rain set in. Ominous dark clouds loomed overhead.

Kylie frowned, as she led the way outside. She wished she'd not agreed to join her friends. Alan Titchmarsh made it seem so simple on TV. This looked like it was going to be hard graft. She'd come to support her friend though, so she had to bite the bullet. She took out a pair of gardening shears nestled at the back of George's shed and wasted no time. She went straight to it, hacking away at the overgrown weeds.

"I'll do the mowing," Rachel said. "You tackle the weeds, Dotty if you can work out which are weeds and which are flowers."

"That's the six-million- dollar question. Are those weeds?" Dotty pointed at a cluster of dandelions.

"You've got to be kidding me." Rachel put her hands on her hips and looked across at her friend.

"Yes, I am. Even I know they need to come out." Dotty slid her long slender hands in the green gardening gloves. As always, Dotty had dressed more to impress than for practical reasons. She wore a gingham blouse, gathered and tied in a bow at the front. With her cropped dungarees and scarf in her hair tied up in a bow on her crown, she looked more like a land girl. Knowing Dotty, she would soon be daydreaming about what life was like for those women who helped on farms during the war. She set about with a trowel.

Using as much force as she was able, she dug up the hardy yellow flowers.

The other two girls were busy doing their share when suddenly Dotty let out a mighty scream and ran towards the back of the large garden.

"Whatever's the matter, Dotty?"

"Worms," she said, "Loads of them."

"They won't harm you."

"No, I can't go back there. I'm scared." She raised a gloved wrist to her forehead as she spoke.

"Whoever heard of a gardener scared of worms." Rachel shook her head. "Here, I'll take over. Somehow, I don't think this will work. I can do the hoeing and you turn the soil over by those roses over there. I've checked it out — it's a worm-free zone. The roses will need manure putting round them once you've dug them over."

"Oh no, not manure," Dotty said.

"What's wrong with manure, Dotty?" Rachel asked.

"It's messy, and it smells." The other two girls looked at each other and shook their heads. It was very doubtful that Dotty would make a gardener at this rate. Dotty pulled a face but continued to work without incident. The odd ouch and huff could be heard as Dotty pricked her finger on a thorny rose bush.

She threw a stick for Winnie which was a big mistake. It meant she couldn't get anything done because Winnie kept retrieving it and coming back for more. She stayed at Dotty's heels and got under her feet as she put her foot on the edge of the spade.

"Lie down, Winnie. There's a good girl," she said in the sickly soft voice she always used on Winnie. She could never shout at her with those doleful doggy eyes. She threw the stick over the other side of the garden again, but Winnie found an interest in something else. The poodle began to dig, accompanied by a series of high-pitched yelps.

The other two were oblivious to what was going on. They had got into the swing of their tasks. Kylie hummed away as she worked.

Suddenly, a blood-curdling cry rang out. It came from the corner of the garden where Dotty was working. Rachel wondered what she had done this time. Knowing Dotty, she had probably stabbed her toe with the spade. Kylie downed tools and went over to where her friend stood.

Dotty's face had turned a pale grey colour.

"Whatever's the matter, Dotty? Another worm?"

Dotty's hand trembled. Kylie frowned and followed the route to where her gaze had locked.

"What is it, Dotty?" Rachel asked. Dotty rubbed her eyes in disbelief.

"What have you found?" Kylie questioned. Dotty did a double-take, then scratched her jaw. Her expression blanched.

"I don't believe it," she said. She shook her head. Her mouth was wide open.

"You don't believe what?" Kylie questioned.

"Look there. See what Winnie and I have unearthed."

"What is it?" Rachel peered over the edge of the spade.

"Well, I'll be."

The three girls slumped their bodies forward unable to unlock their eyes as they scrutinized what lay on the ground. Rachel bent to pick up Dotty's find.

Chapter 4

"It might be a dog's bones or another animal," Dotty said. Her eyes were fixed on the grisly discovery.

"No, that's a human head." Rachel began to poke around the area with a stick.

"Trust me to find something like this. I feel sick." Dotty looked across at her friends for sympathy.

"It's exciting. I mean, it's not every day you find a dead body in your garden."

"Kylie! We're not at Fred West's house." Rachel frowned at her friend who was known for putting her foot in it and saying the wrong things.

Only the crown of the skull poked above the disturbed soil. It was a tiny body. The girls froze to the spot. They knew they should leave the corpse alone, but human nature being what it was, they were a nosey trio. They couldn't help themselves from prodding away and continuing to search.

Dotty held what she thought was an arm, then pushed it back into the soil. She lifted her dog out of the way. Winnie was keen to explore some more and didn't take kindly to being moved. Her continuous barking didn't help the stress caused by the situation. Kylie knelt and removed the earth from around the skull. She wasn't religious, but she made a hasty cross over her chest.

"I remember seeing a skeleton once in Biology. That was scary enough, and it was only plastic."

"We shouldn't touch anything else," Dotty said. She wrestled with Winnie who tried with all her might to free herself from Dotty's clutches. "We need to call the police. How long do you think the bones have been there?" The three girls stopped what they were doing as it dawned on them what finding a dead body in George's garden could mean.

"I don't know but I wonder if Grandad George knows anything about this?" Rachel looked across at the kitchen window. Her grandad was sat inside watching snooker on TV, oblivious to what was going on in his garden. She knew when he was told what they had discovered, he wouldn't be happy. Not because there was a body in the garden. He would no longer be able to sit cheering on Ronnie the Rocket. He would have to leave his nest. It may mean him spending time at the police station. He would moan about that. Missing a frame of the world championships would make him grumpy. If he had to miss a whole match to speak to the police, he would be mortified.

Rachel recalled an occasion when the Shanghai Masters tournament was on. Grandad George had an upset tummy and needed to spend forever in the bathroom with the runs. He missed John Higgins' maximum break. He watched it many times on replay since, but he said that wasn't the same as being there the moment it happened. Being there for George, meant being transfixed to the TV screen. George wouldn't dream of spending money going up to the Crucible in Sheffield to watch any tournaments live, however much he loved snooker. The family never heard the last of him missing the momentous match though. He even continued to moan about it while they sat eating their Christmas dinner that year. They got all the gory details of his upset stomach as they attempted to tuck into their turkey dinners. Food got wasted thanks to Grandad George explicitly recapping on the occasion.

The wind was getting up and Winnie became distracted by a plastic bag that had danced along the grass and settled in one of the rose bushes. Dotty knew she couldn't continue to restrain her pet for any length of time. To leave her outside could prove disastrous.

"Come on. Let's go inside and make a cup of tea. We shouldn't touch anything out here. I'll give the police a ring and put the kettle on." Tea was always the order of the day in a crisis. This was a crisis on a bigger scale than Dotty had known before.

The last major incident she could remember was when Kylie's dad ran off with one of the young bar staff where Kylie worked. On that occasion, the three girls turned detective. They found where the couple shacked up. They had absconded to a canal boat to live on the Thames. Kylie had been so angry with her dad, she plotted how she could sink his boat. When her friends wouldn't support her in carrying out the dastardly deed, she chickened out and went home. At least she was happy in the fact her dad froze his nuts off in the middle of winter when the barge had no heating. He had to rely on his love to keep him warm. Needless to say, the relationship didn't last through that cold harsh winter. He tried to return home, his tail between his legs, but Kylie's mum, Jan, would heat nothing of it.

Rachel decided to leave it to the police to tell her grandad about their discovery. She didn't want to be shot as the messenger of bad news. She had no intentions of being the one to stop George watching his beloved snooker.

"That was quick work, girls. Have you finished already?" George's concept of time was confused. They hadn't been outside long enough to scratch the surface of what needed doing.

"No, we thought we'd come inside for a break. The sky's looking dodgy. Rain could be on the way," Dotty said as she sat stroking her dog.

"Fair weather workers, are you? That wouldn't have happened in my day." The three girls looked at each other. Dotty wondered how George would react when he heard their news. Her stomach churned as she thought about the small collection of bones lying in the garden. Did George know anything about the skeleton? How long must it have been there? Was George the one who buried it? The idea was too unthinkable to imagine. But they had to face facts. Nobody had a dead body in their garden without raising suspicion on themselves.

For all they knew, they could be sitting next to a killer.

Chapter 5

"So, if you can describe in your own words how you came by the discovery, Miss Drinkwater." The lanky policeman with a spotty complexion looked at his notepad, licked the tip of his pencil, then waited, hand poised for Dotty's reply.

"Well, the three of us and Winnie had started tackling George's garden."

"Can I interrupt you there, who's Winnie?"

"Winnie the poodle, my dog."

"Aah, I see. Carry on."

"I'd settled into doing some digging after I'd finished throwing sticks for Winnie."

"Quite." The policeman blew out a big sigh.

"I was over by the roses. The soil needed turning over. You know how it is." That was a white lie. Rachel had informed her. "Those roses needed feeding with manure to be at their best." Dotty tried to sound like a competent gardener who knew her stuff when in reality she didn't know her onions from her begonias.

"Get to the point, please." Dotty frowned. She'd wanted to impart her newfound knowledge about all things horticultural on someone. Anyone would have done but obviously, the police had more important business to concern themselves with than George's roses.

"I put my foot on the spade and the blade hit something firm. Winnie was sniffing around, so I had to tread carefully. There was a resounding thunk. Intrigued, Winnie and I proceeded to clear away the overlying soil. Well, it was mainly Winnie. She's good at that sort of thing."

"I'll bear that in mind if ever I need a dog to dig up any dead bodies for me. Go on." Dotty couldn't tell if the police officer was being facetious.

"I bent down for a closer look because I hoped it may be buried treasure we'd unearthed, but there it was, as clear as day, a skeleton."

"I see." The policeman scribbled in his notepad.

"I may have peered in to get a more accurate inspection but as soon as I realised what it was, I scarpered."

"That's right, officer. Dotty screamed, and we both came running over, didn't we Kylie?" Rachel nodded. Dotty frowned and glared at her. Rachel was sat with her chin dipped and a slumped posture. She looked like a guilty person. Kylie was even worse. She averted her eyes and couldn't look at any of us.

"Nobody touched anything, honestly," Kylie said, keen to show that her friend shouldn't be incriminated in any way. George's loud outburst made everyone jump.

"You found a skeleton?"

"That's right, Grandad." Rachel patted his arm as if to say, don't concern yourself. The fact was that George should be very concerned. It wasn't every day human remains were discovered in your garden. To make matters worse, a spider chose that moment to scurry across the carpet and Kylie let out a heart rendering cry.

Dotty ran out of the room. She rushed into the kitchen and waited for the coast to clear. Spiders were worse than worms, in her world. She glanced out the window. Members of the police force had arrived and were milling around the garden. The doorbell rang, and she went to answer.

"Detective Sergeant Kevin Windsor from CID, ma'am. No relation to Elizabeth." He held out his ID card. Dotty stared at it and frowned.

"Elizabeth?" she queried.

"The Queen, ma'am, the Queen." He laughed but Dotty didn't find it funny. Her stress levels struggled when there was too much going on and her discovery had put paid to any likelihood of a quiet afternoon.

"You'd better come through."

Grandad George was in a daze. He hadn't turned the TV off, but he couldn't hear anything with all the noise his unwelcome guests made.

"What's going on?" he asked.

"There's been an unfortunate set of bones found in your garden, George."

It wasn't too long before the detective sergeant gave them an update on the situation.

"The skeleton appears to have been there some time. The age of the bones will determine if there are any requirements for an investigation. We'll be seeking the assistance of anthropologists to establish how long they have been there. We may have to use carbon dating techniques to put an age on them. In the meantime, we need to carry out inquiries."

George suddenly sat bolt upright in his chair and did something unheard of. He picked up the remote control and turned off the TV.

"So, I've got a graveyard in my back garden that I never knew about. Will I be on the telly?"

"You could be Grandad George. It depends on what the police find."

"In that case, I need to get my hair cut. Have you seen how untidy it is at the back?" He patted the back of his head. "Do you still have the number for that mobile hairdresser, Rachel?"

"I'll do better than that, Grandad. If you tell me where your clippers are, I will do it for you."

"What? Now?"

"There's no time like the present."

"They're in the bathroom cabinet."

Five minutes later, George was sat with a towel wrapped around his body and Rachel poised to start the cut. She hadn't cut her grandad's hair before, but she had shaved her boyfriend Marvin's on several occasions. She imagined herself as something of a hairdresser and it saved him money on the High street barbers whose prices had doubled in the past year. Her grandad liked a short back and sides, so his style was straightforward. Rachel used her judgement and considering she hadn't done his hair previously, she didn't do a bad job, even if she said so herself.

DS Kevin Windsor – no relation to the Queen had been waiting in the wings to interview George. He looked on and laughed.

"I've questioned people before who've insisted on getting dressed first because they were still in their nightclothes, but I've never come across anyone who needed a haircut first."

"All done, Grandad," Rachel said as she brushed the hair off his shoulders and pulled up the sheet she put down to collect the white hair.

"I hope Mavis likes it." George visited the nursing home where his wife lived every day. They were both creatures of habit. Her dementia meant she didn't know if he turned up morning, noon or night. George, however, was as regimented as a soldier and arrived at 2 pm on the dot. This king of routine caught the bus outside his front door and only had a short walk once he got off. It was as well because he struggled to walk with his aches and pains. With George, his mind was still active. It was his body that let him down.

His wife, Mavis had left her youth behind like a purse lost down the sofa. Her memory faded many years ago and the pair of them tried to cope with her forgetfulness and confusion for longer than was good for either of them. George struggled to come to terms with his wife's illness. He got angry and frustrated with her when she kept putting the keys in the oven, or the bathroom cabinet, or the wardrobe. She put them everywhere but where they belonged on the hook in the hall. Before she moved into the home, they spent their days looking for keys and glasses and purses. They looked for just about everything. Searching for their belongings became their main focus in life.

Now Mavis was being cared for, George could get back to doing what he liked best — watching TV and listening to country and western music on the radio. He'd been sad when Mavis went in and had to admit that he found life difficult. He still missed her, but it wasn't all bad. There were some bonuses. He no longer had to endure Emmerdale and Doctors. Now his favourite granddaughter, Rachel came to see him and help around the house every week. No, life wasn't bad at all, apart from this pesky disturbance. Who on earth could have buried a body in his garden, he wondered? That was what the detective sergeant wanted to know. George couldn't throw any light on the matter.

"So, you've no idea who the missing bones could belong to?" George was asked for the umpteenth time. He was beginning to believe these police officers may have dementia like Mavis. They kept asking the same questions over and over. Thankfully, they finished with him before he lost his rag.

After everyone left, and the remains had been dug up and packaged off for testing, Rachel stayed to chat to her grandad.

"Have you any thoughts on who the bones could belong to, Grandad?"

George scratched his chin and peered at her.

"I hope it was nothing to do with the time Mavis went soft on the young man from the travelling fair."

"What do you mean?" Rachel looked at him, her eyes as wide as saucers.

"What do you think I mean?" he sneered.

"Are you saying that Nana Mavis had an affair?"

His face remained blank.

"I'm not saying anything. You work it out for yourself."

Chapter 6

Dotty's new gardening business had come to an abrupt halt. The girls called an extraordinary meeting to discuss recent events. They drove over to Horsham to the cocktail bar there to avoid any prying eyes or wagging ears. What they had to say was for their ears only.

"When word of this gets out, there's going to be all sorts of speculation." Rachel ordered the drinks.

"We mustn't jump to conclusions. Those bones could date back to Roman times. Your grandparents might not be guilty," Dotty said. She had driven them over, so now sat nursing a glass of coke.

"Never mind that, you ought to have some business cards printed up. You could cash in on the publicity Rachel's grandad will get." Kylie munched on a packet of cheese and onion crisps.

"That's rather mercenary. Those bones belong to someone's loved one." Dotty frowned.

"She's right, though. It's what all the top companies do. They say that even bad publicity is worth having. You could make a fortune out of this, Dotty." Rachel helped herself to one of Kylie's crisps.

"Hey, they're mine." Kylie snatched the packet out of reach.

"Come on, Kylie, just one. Don't be tight."

"Stop squabbling girls. There are serious issues to discuss here."

"That's true. Have you thought of a name for your new venture, Dotty?" Rachel asked.

"How about Lawn and order?" Kylie chomped away. Dotty laughed.

"I like that idea. I don't plan to do more than cut the grass for a few of the pensioners in the area."

"At least you won't have to do Grandad's garden now. It looks as though the police are digging that up. I just hope they don't make a mess."

"Or find any more bodies." Dotty shivered.

"So, on a serious note, what do you make of your grandad's comments? Do you think he knows anything about the discovery?" Kylie screwed up the empty packet and squashed it into the ashtray.

"I believe my grandad." Rachels' mouth turned down at the ends.

"We need to see what the bone expert finds and what the DNA results reveal before we go jumping to any conclusions."

"I reckon it's your nana Mavis who is the murderer and not your grandad," Kylie said it in such a matter-of-fact way, the other two girls looked over her in shock.

"Kylie!" they said in unison.

"Keep your voice down," Rachel whispered.

"No one's about." Kylie held her arm aloft and fanned it around the room.

"That's not the point. Rachel's grandparents could be in serious trouble. We need to find out what we can about that incident from your nana's past." Dotty did speech marks in the air with her fingers at the mention of the word incident.

"Good idea. If she had a fling years ago, we don't want the neighbours gossiping unnecessarily. We should find out about that travelling fair, especially if Grandad suspects Nana of cheating on him.

"Talking of cheats, how is Marvin?" Kylie smiled at Rachel. Rachel glared back at her. She didn't reply. Kylie assumed that things weren't good between them. "Has he been at it again?"

"I don't know." Rachel's shoulders slumped, and she looked down at the table.

"You know the saying — once a cheat, always a cheat."

"Thanks for that, Kylie. I don't need reminding."

"The trouble with you Rachel, you rush into relationships before you've discovered what they are like. You see a hunky guy and you're smitten. I mean, look what happened when you were wed to Steve."

"Dotty's right. Your wedding cake lasted longer than your marriage."

"Stop ganging up on me."

"We're not. We're only trying to help. You won't listen to advice, anyway. The trouble with you is that you wait until you've had a load of pain before you change anything. You must admit that Marvin's got a roving eye." Dotty cocked her head to one side. She felt sorry for her friend, but Rachel never seemed to learn her lesson when it came to men. They walked all over her and she let them. It was sad because she was such a lovely girl.

"It goes with the territory. His job doesn't help." Rachel's mouth took a downward turn.

"What, because he's a window cleaner? Not all window cleaners jump into bed with every pretty young thing they come into contact with." Kylie shook her head.

"It's only when he gets drunk that he strays."

"Only!" Kylie said, looking at the others. Dotty shrugged her shoulders. There was no hope for Rachel. She couldn't see what was as plain as day — Marvin was a waste of space.

"Oh no, have you seen who's just walked in?" Rachel was facing the door. The other two needed to turn around to see who it was. It was impossible to do it discreetly. Kylie tried to turn slowly. She moved her body round in a circle like a cuckoo clock that needed winding up.

"Holy Moly, it's him again." She hunched her shoulders and swerved her frame back into the circle with her friends. Dotty didn't look round. She didn't want to make it so obvious that they were talking about whoever it was.

"What? Who is it?" she whispered.

"It's your neighbour, Hans, again. He's here with his bit of stuff."

Hans and his lady friend walked towards them. Because the girls were stood at the bar, he couldn't avoid bumping into them. Dotty and the others nodded at him.

"This is Greta, my colleague." Rachel and Dotty had turned into nodding dogs.

"Very nice." Kylie looked her up and down. Rachel nudged her before she put her foot in it like she normally did. Kylie opened her mouth to say something, but Dotty stood on her toe. "Ow." Kylie frowned at her friend who couldn't wait to pull her away from this awkward situation.

Greta was either brazen or seemed oblivious to the stir she was causing. Hans, on the other hand, looked uncomfortable. He bounced from foot to foot and tried to move up the bar to get served. Greta tottered after him in her six-inch-high heels. The girls' eyes followed her ample derriere which was clad in a dark brown leather mini skirt. She placed her tongue on the top of her lip and ran it around the rim of her mouth. Her bright coral lipstick didn't budge an inch.

As soon as the couple had moved on and were out of hearing range, Kylie turned to her friends.

"Arrogant little hussy. What a cheek! Bringing his bit on the side in here."

"I wonder if his wife knows?" Dotty said.

"I doubt it but even if she did, I can't imagine her being thrilled about it. I wouldn't be if my husband made a fool of himself like that." The other two thought how inapt Rachel's words were. They fitted Rachel's situation to a tee. Her ex-husband had paraded his secret affair around in the same way. It hadn't taken long before Rachel found out about her.

Her history with men had knocked her confidence and self-esteem. Virtually every man she cared about had cheated on her. Two of them returned to their ex-girlfriends. One time, she was seeing a guy who was estranged from his wife and he ended up wanting to make another go of his marriage. It got to the stage where Rachel felt she should set up a marriage guidance bureau. If anyone wanted to patch up their relationship, all they had to do was spend three months with her and they went running back to their exes.

She looked across where Hans and Greta sat. Her friends joined her in glaring at the couple. Hans and Greta weren't cuddling or smooching or doing anything wildly romantic. The girls opened their eyes wide in disbelief. Dotty rubbed hers.

Hans and Greta sipped their pints of lager. Greta had put on a pair of glasses and the two of them were studying some paperwork. Very strange! It wasn't the sort of behaviour you'd expect from a bimbo and her German lover.

Chapter 7

"We ought to go and see your nana," Kylie said, biting into a Mars bar. Rachel swallowed in quick succession several times. She knew she didn't visit her nana as often as she should.

"Have the police spoken to her yet?" Dotty asked.

"I don't think so, but Grandad avoids the question when I ask him. He is highly embarrassed by the whole affair. A lady from the newspaper approached him the other day."

"Blast, we should have got Dotty in on it to talk about her gardening business."

"My mum took over. She was trying to protect him from too much media attention."

"It's not gone viral though, has it?"

"No, but it can't be pleasant for him. He's lived in the same house for most of his married life. He's never had a cross word with any of the neighbours. I tell a lie, there was that time when Gordon next door chopped some of Grandad's sycamore tree down that overhung into his garden. Grandad went mad. Now, all the neighbours will be talking about him, especially Betty Simpson. You know what she's like. She's a right gossip."

Two days later, the three girls stood outside the nursing home where Nana Mavis lived. As the front door opened, and they got a whiff from inside, Rachel remembered why she didn't come here as often as she would like. It was mainly the smell that put her off. Kylie called it the pee palace which seemed appropriate, given the unpleasant smells wafting up her nostrils. If you arrived here after a heavy meal, you would be likely to bring it back up. It wasn't cheap to stay here either. All Rachel's grandparents' savings, where they had scrimped and done without holidays for years to get by now had to go on Nana Mavis's lodgings.

The cost riled Rachel. Mainly because it was unlikely that there would be any savings left as inheritance money for her. The family did what they could to look after Nana Mavis, but it was an impossible task. She kept going wandering. The police were forever bringing her back. They were at her home most weeks, either them or the ambulance people. If she didn't go missing, she fell over or did something stupid. She once tried to climb the tree in the back garden looking for Polly, the cat that had been dead for twenty years. George was on first-name terms with the local constabulary. They had been to his home so many times, he knew all their family members now.

As they parked their car, they spotted Nana Mavis. She sat in her customary spot, by the window looking out. She looked so peaceful with her snowy white hair and craggy features. Rachel wondered how much she knew about where she was. Did she know what had happened to her? It crucified her grandad, especially in the beginning. At least, it did until he invested in his new TV. Now he found comfort in watching what he wanted when he wanted.

Rachel was told that people with dementia liked to reminisce about things in their distant past because it was the short-term memory where they struggled. Because of that, she often turned up with a photo album or some keepsake from days gone by. This time she brought nothing other than her two friends. A member of staff led them through the hallway with its high ceiling and ornate panelling. She opened the dark brown door. It creaked but didn't drown out the sound of her voice as she shouted across the room.

"Mavis, you've got visitors." Everyone looked up. There were one or two family members sat with other residents dotted around the lounge between the commodes and zimmer frames. The girls bounced over the paisley swirled carpet in the large drawing-room towards the bay window. A lady called Agnes grabbed hold of Rachel's arm and asked her the same question she asked every time she saw her.

"Is my daughter coming to visit today?" The first time she asked, Rachel looked around for help from one of the staff members. Since then, they had chatted many times, so she knew what to say.

"She'll be here to see you soon, Agnes."

"Oh, not today then?" Agnes seemed upset. She frowned, with her shoulders drooped.

"No, not today."

"Oh dear, I thought she would be here today." It would probably be a lot of todays before Agnes only relative, her daughter Anne visited. She lived in Australia. She had flown over once in the three years that Agnes lived in the home. Rachel felt a pang of sadness every time she spoke to her. Life could be so cruel.

The lady sat at the table in front of Mavis collared the girls.

"Don't listen to Henry," she said.

"We won't," Rachel replied.

"Not a word of truth comes out of that man's mouth. It's not right. He shouldn't be allowed in. Calls himself a Member of Parliament, I don't know who he thinks he is." The friends didn't have a clue who the lady was talking about, but Rachel had learnt how to humour them.

"It's okay, we won't be voting for him," she said.

Mavis smiled as the girls approached but her eyes were vacant. After greeting Mavis, they went to sit down, but their attention was diverted to a commotion over the other side of the room. Everyone looked to see what the noise was.

"Come on, sit back down, Albert. That sandwich is for eating not throwing," a worried-looking staff member said. She tried to put her arm around Albert's shoulder. He shrugged her off and stamped his feet.

"I don't want to eat it. It's not fit for human consumption. Even the ducks would turn their noses up at that shite."

"Albert, mind your language. There are ladies and guests present."

"They're no ladies. They're whores, every last one of them." He shouted at the top of his voice. The people sat around glared at him dumbfounded. Another member of staff went over to Albert in support of her colleague. Together, they did their best to calm him down. Kylie laughed. This was better than watching any comedy sketch on TV.

"Never a dull moment, eh?" she said as she perched herself in a tall-backed chair. Rachel tried hard to ignore the disturbance and talk to her nana.

"How's your sandwich, Nana?" she asked, speaking loudly. Even with her hearing aid in, Mavis struggled to hear.

"It's very nice, dear," Mavis said as she chewed and chewed. Chewing took a long time because she had taken her dentures out to eat it.

"Wouldn't you be better putting your false teeth back in, Nana?" Rachel felt uncomfortable with the sight of the teeth on top of the table.

"No, dear. I can't eat with them in. They're too painful. They're only for show." Rachel nodded and made a mental note to speak to someone about Mavis's dentures. She sighed. Every time she visited, her Nana's health needed attention. From broken glasses to her hearing aid going missing, there was always something to deal with. This growing old was no fun.

A member of staff brought tea for them and the girls watched as Mavis's shaky frail hands reached for her cup. The trembling continued so Rachel cupped her hand around the plastic mug that was given to Mavis. She waited until her nana took a sip and put the hot tea safely back on the tray.

Rachel introduced her friends to her nana. They had met on many occasions before, but she knew that Mavis would say they hadn't. To avoid any embarrassment, she always introduced them again. After the niceties were over, Rachel asked her nana a few questions.

"Nana, do you ever remember the travelling fair coming to town?"

Mavis looked out of the window for a few moments then turned towards her granddaughter and smiled.

"Oh yes," she said. "That was where I met Paddy."

Rachel had been told by her mother that she came from good stock. Rachel's mother liked to think she verged on being a member of the aristocracy. That seemed far-fetched to Rachel, as her grandad was from the east end of London. Nana Mavis though had come from a wealthy lineage. Her great grandpapa was reputed to be an earl. Rachel hadn't researched it, although she believed he had once been mayor of London. Now, a disconcerting thought came over her. If her nana had got together with this guy, Paddy, then it was possible that she had gypsy blood rather than blue blood. That would mean she had Irish travelling descent. She wasn't so sure she wanted to find out any more about her Nana's philandering.

Chapter 8

Dotty grew up with the attitude of wanting to save the world. It stemmed from watching superheroes on TV. She couldn't even blame her brother, Joe for her obsession with Superman and Batman. She had been keen on superheroes long before Joe was born. Dotty wanted to be Supergirl and Batgirl rolled into one. The idea of walking into a phone box, doing a twirl and coming out with superpowers had been another thing she daydreamed about for years. Nowadays, being a superhero came out lower down the pecking order of priorities. Making cupcakes, knitting and sewing her own clothes were how Dotty found enjoyment in life. She loved to bake and these days her daydream was to be a good enough baker to meet Paul Hollywood and be a contestant on the *Great British Bake Off*. If she could do it dressed as Supergirl, then she could kill two birds with one stone.

Her mind wandered, then snapped back into the day. Today's focus was on how she could help Rachel prove her nana couldn't be the person responsible for the human remains in the garden. To clear Mavis's name, Dotty had gone along with Rachel to visit Mavis's oldest friend, Audrey.

They'd walked up the path of Audrey's bungalow and rang the bell. They waited but no one arrived. Rachel rapped on the door frame. Still nothing. Suddenly, they heard a crashing noise coming from the back garden.

"Aargh," came the sound of Audrey's voice. They ran around the side of the house. Luckily the back gate was open. Audrey lay on the ground, a washing line filled with underwear covered her face and body.

"Audrey? Whatever happened? Can you move? Is there anything broken?" From the way Audrey thrashed her arms and legs about, it was obvious she had no broken bones.

"Get me out of here. This bloomin' washing line attacked me." The plastic line had entwined around Audrey's body and she wrestled to free herself. She spat a pair of oversized bloomers out of her mouth. Rachel and Dotty went to her rescue and unravelled her then slowly got her into a garden chair.

"What happened, Audrey?" Rachel asked. A small overturned step stool lay next to her.

"I was hanging out the washing. I've been told not to climb. My knees gave way. It's my own fault, but if I don't use the step, I can't reach the washing line. It's a plague being so small." Audrey was tiny in height, but she wasn't petite. Her girth was almost as wide as her body was long. "It's a good job I'm not going out anywhere. Look at the state of me."

Audrey now had grass stains and dirt from the soil on her pink skirt. Dotty helped to brush her down, then linked her arm and led her into the house. Before long the three of them were sat drinking tea and having a good old chin wag. Rachel knew that most old people liked to talk about the olden days so before she broached the subject of her nana's indiscretions, she asked Audrey about her past.

"I'm a few years older than your nana. In fact, I think I'm older than George."

"So, do you remember the war?" Rachel engaged Audrey in conversation.

"That bloomin' Hitler has a lot to answer for. It's his fault I suffer with my nerves today."

"Why is that then?" Dotty asked.

"Bombing everywhere like he did. Do you know he bombed our chippy? I can't tell you how scary it was, every time I heard a plane flying over. All the family thought we were for the high jump. The trouble was that associating a plane flying overhead meant I got nervous that we would be bombed, even up to a few years ago. Those air raid sirens put the fear of God into me." Dotty nodded. She couldn't imagine having to cope with anything as frightening as the blitz in London. She shuddered when she considered the stories she had been told about lives lost in the war.

"You've been friends with Nana for a long time, haven't you?" Dotty was glad that Rachel had changed the subject.

"Yes dear, we were at school together. My parents lived across the road from Mavis. In those days, when you got married you couldn't afford your own property, so we both moved in with our parents when we were wed. We go back a long way."

"You must miss her now she's in the nursing home?"

"I do dear, but I've lost so many friends. I have to grin and bear it. I'm lucky to still be here at my age. I thank him every day."

"You thank who?"

"God, of course."

"Yes, of course.

"That's a terrible how d'you do, that discovery at Mavis and George's place, isn't it?"

"Yes, and they believe it to be human bones. Have you any theories about it?"

"The body probably dates back to when the king was on the throne," Audrey suggested.

"Maybe, but they weren't that deep. Dotty made the gruesome find."

"Poor dear." Audrey cocked her head to the left and turned her lips down at the sides.

"Audrey?" Rachel moved closer right up to Audrey's left ear.

"Yes, dear?"

"I've got a personal question I would like to ask you about my nana."

"What's that, dear?"

"Do you know if she ever cheated on Grandad?" Audrey grinned.

"Don't let any notions like that trickle into that pretty little head of yours."

"It's important you are honest, Audrey." Dotty's strait-laced approach made Audrey sit up and listen.

"We found out about Paddy," Rachel said.

"I see." Audrey spoke slowly and nodded.

"What can you tell us about him?" Dotty asked. It felt like they were playing good cop, bad cop and she took the tougher no-nonsense approach.

"Well, he was Irish."

"Yes, carry on." The girls leaned forward closer to Audrey.

"He was fond of poteen, you know, the home-made Irish whisky. Trouble was when he drank it, he used to see leprechauns and goblins dancing round.

"So, it sent him loopy?" Dotty asked.

"It did that." Audrey nodded.

"And was Nana romantically involved with him?" Audrey glanced from one girl to the other.

"It isn't my place to say. True friends never gossip about each other. Did you know that she met Paddy after she was married to George?"

"Yes, I'd worked that out, but with her dementia, I can't ask her questions about it and it could be important in light of recent developments."

"So, you want to know if they were making whoopee?"

"Sorry?" Rachel frowned.

"You are asking me if they made hay together or turned over in the cabbage patch?"

"Err, yeah, I suppose so."

"I think the modern expression is — were they doing bits? As far as I know, they did it once then Mavis got cold feet or decided that George was a better catch than a man who moved around the country with his travelling fair. Paddy probably had a lady in every town. Plus, the drinking didn't help. Paddy was a few sandwiches short of a picnic when he supped a drop of the Irish."

"I see." Dotty stroked Rachel's arm. It looked like Mavis had a guilty secret. That wasn't the news that Rachel wanted to hear.

Chapter 9

"So, get this," said Dotty as she bit into her crushed avocado sandwich. "I've been reading on the internet that if you upload a baby's DNA to a genealogy website, forensic genealogists can match it up with the mother."

"Oh dear, I hope those bones aren't linked to Nana Mavis. I would hate her to go to prison." Rachel swirled the spoon around the froth on the top of her mug of latte and took a sip.

"They're not likely to put her in prison. She isn't mentally capable," Kylie said as her mouth opened wide and she devoured the cream cake in front of her.

"Think of the shame it would cause poor Grandad."

"You are jumping to conclusions. Wait until we find out what the police discover." Dotty licked her fingers and wiped the corner of her lips with them.

"You've got to admit that it's not looking good for Mavis. It's unlikely that anyone else would dump a body in your grandparent's garden."

Dotty looked across the table at her friend. Kylie was prone to weeding out the negative in situations. Right now, her comments weren't helping Rachel's family crisis.

"My mum hasn't slept a wink since Dotty found those bones. I wish we'd never agreed to help Grandad with his garden."

"You can't go blaming Dotty. It's not her fault she's unearthed a murder."

"A murder!" Rachel looked horrified. "We don't know that a murder has been committed."

"Oh, come on, don't be naïve. There's no other reason human remains would be found buried." Kylie leaned her right elbow on top of the other arm and slid a finger up by her cheek, her other fingers rested on her chin. She pursed her lips together.

"Winnie and I must take the blame. Talking of which, I'm just going to see if she's alright tied up outside."

Dotty went to check on her dog. An old man stopped to stroke her, and Dotty chatted with him about various breeds of dogs before she returned to her friends in the café. Marcella, the café owner told Dotty that Winnie was allowed inside but Dotty didn't like to encroach on her hospitality in case other customers weren't as understanding. She didn't intend to stay too long today as she had jobs to do, the first of which was taking Winnie for a walk.

The girls came to the Strawberry tea rooms every Saturday afternoon come rain or shine. It was a ritual that started in their final school year and they only cancelled if one of them was ill or they were on holiday. The plan originally was to help with their revision. It didn't work. They talked about anything but schoolwork — boys, clothes, makeup. None of them had done very well at school and only Rachel had gone to college to do an administrative course. She couldn't understand why you needed qualifications to file papers and run to the shop for her manager. She had the best job out of the three of them. She hoped that one day she would earn enough to afford the deposit on her own place rather than renting. The alternative was she would meet Mr Right with a wad of money to keep her. Something told her it wouldn't be Marvin.

"Oh, I could eat another of those." Kylie wolfed down the first cream cake and was now eyeing up a chocolate éclair.

"Think of your figure," Rachel said.

"It's alright for you Miss Skin and Bone. I just look at a cake and I put on half a stone."

"From where I'm sitting, you've been doing more than looking at them." Kylie glared at Rachel.

"A girl has to have some pleasures in life, and I can't find myself a suitable fella. Don't you agree, Dotty?" Both Dotty and Kylie were single. Watching Rachel's disasters with men was enough to put them off.

"You ought to follow Dotty's example. How much is that you've lost now, Dotty?"

"Two kilograms." Dotty liked to weigh herself in kilograms because she couldn't work out how heavy she was the same as she could in stones and pounds. To her, eighty-three kg sounded better than 183lbs or thirteen stone. Thirteen stone! She'd never been that heavy in all her years of overindulging on chocolate and chips. Thirteen stone was the magic figure that prompted her into action. She quickly changed the bathroom scales over to kilograms and immediately she didn't feel as bad.

This alarming discovery had called for drastic measures. She tried omitting breakfast for a week but that hadn't worked. By noon each day, she was ravenous enough to eat a scabby horse. She ate everything in sight. Since then she had researched other diets. She wasn't new to the weight-loss scene. She battled with her weight from her teens and had tried many diets along the way. There was Weightwatchers, Slimming World, the Cambridge diet, Atkins, the Mayo clinic and Slimfast. By doing these different diets, she found out something very important. She made a profound discovery about herself. The outcome of these dieting failures had taught her some very vital lessons. One was that she couldn't stick to a diet and two — she loved food, especially chocolate.

Dotty woke up thinking about food and went to bed each night dreaming about her next meal. She loved cooking and had a library of recipe books. Her TV viewing consisted of watching all the cookery shows. She had become a competent baker and loved making artisan bread. For her eighteenth birthday, she received a breadmaking machine off her family. It might not have been the normal present to give a young girl, but Dotty was no ordinary girl. The excitement she felt when she used it the first time was nothing short of sublime. She put the ingredients in the machine and left it overnight to do its worst. The following morning, when she got up, she popped her head in to look inside the breadmaker, there it was! Voila — a loaf of bread had appeared as if by magic. The smell was divine, and Dotty was like a kid on Christmas morning, jumping for joy.

"Oh, pooh," Kylie said as she scooped up the chocolate spread that dropped onto her blouse. She hadn't been able to resist that enticing chocolate éclair. Rachel's words had spurred her on to want more rather than deter her. "So, what diet are you doing now?" she asked her friend.

"I'm trying not to think about the psychology of being on a diet. If I tell myself I am on a diet, by my record, I will fail. Somehow, the word diet makes me feel like I'm missing out. I get depressed, start feeling sorry for myself and eat more. So, this time I am doing a healthy eating plan."

"Sounds the same thing to me. If it's good for you, I don't like it. Cottage cheese — yuck. Cucumber — waste of time. And if it's bad for you, I love it. I'll stick with my seafood diet."

"What you're on a diet, Kylie?"

"Yes, I see food and I eat it."

"Ha, bloody ha."

"Anyway, guys, I've no more news so if we've no one else to gossip about then I'm off. I'll speak to you soon." Dotty rose from the chair and kissed both her friends twice. This continental style of greeting had now caught on in the UK thanks to cheap European travel.

They said their goodbyes and Dotty weaved through the seats and walked outside to untie Winnie. She looked so cute looking up at her owner with those doleful doggy eyes. Dotty often left it for other family members to volunteer to take Winnie out. Now she was trying to lose weight, she hoped the exercise would burn off a few extra calories.

Winnie stayed at Dotty's heels as they walked up the recently refurbished High street and down the lane to the country path. It was only two minutes away from Dotty's home but the countryside around Sussex Weald was spectacular. The main road dated back to Roman times and the village itself had a conservation area at its centre and many beautiful period buildings. The local countryside with its bridle paths and nature trails was an ideal place for Winnie to roam and for Dotty to admire the views.

Winnie was a picture of health. She was well-groomed and had a tail that wagged in appreciation of the attention she got. Dotty let her off the lead while she mooched along through the cornfields. A few minutes later and Winnie leapt through the trees with a large branch in her mouth. Dotty laughed.

"That's too big to throw. Can't you find a smaller one?" Winnie seemed to understand, dropped the one she was carrying and returned to Dotty with a small twig. Dotty hurled it as far as she could and watched as Winnie bounded through the fields after it. They played together for a while.

"Come and get your lead on, Winnie. It's time to go." Winnie took a bit of coaxing. She wanted to play for longer. As Dotty walked Winnie back up her road, she spotted a familiar sight up ahead. Hans was there and had his arm around Greta's shoulder. They hadn't seen Dotty as she was behind them and they had their backs towards her.

Just as Dotty wondered what his wife Molly would make of this liaison, they turned in at his gate. Dotty frowned. Surely, he wasn't taking her home. She scurried along the pavement to see where they went and caught sight of them entering his shed at the side of the house. What were they up to now?

Chapter 10

Two days later and Dotty was still mulling over what she had seen at her neighbour's house or rather the shed of her neighbour, Hans. Taking a work colleague onto his allotment was strange and there was something suspicious about those brown eyes of his. They were set too close together. Dotty realised she shouldn't interfere, but she wanted to warn Molly. If she knew about her husband's behaviour then fair enough, but if she was oblivious to what he was doing, then she had a right to know.

Dotty stood looking in the hall mirror and applied a final coat of her new Rimmel lipstick. She preferred to buy the Tom Ford one but until she started earning real money, such luxuries were out of the question. She dabbed her lips with a tissue, applied a last touch of lip liner and a smidgeon of lip gloss and she was ready. Next, she patted down her fringe which had been stuck up since she got out of bed this morning.

Dotty had made some postcards giving details of her new gardening business. Things may be on hold over at George's for the time being but that didn't stop her looking for more avenues to promote her services. The hairdresser's shop and the café said she could display her cards there. With a bit of luck, she might get a few other business owners to support her cause. She smiled as she thought of herself as a business owner. First stop today was to call on Patsy at the florists. Since Dotty went on a flower arranging course, she now expressed an interest in everything floral. The pair struck up a friendship. Patsy was married to the local vicar and they had two children. She had blue eyes that danced as she spoke. Her thin blonde hair was parted to one side and she tucked it behind her ears.

Dotty wasn't one for that religious stuff. She attended the carol service every Christmas. She also liked to make bread for the harvest when it was Thanksgiving, but other than that, she had no real interest in the church. Being around Patsy, she found it fascinating. If she ignored the fact that Patsy was a clean-living Christian, Dotty would put Patsy in her top three people to spend time with, after her friends Rachel and Kylie. Patsy's dress sense was nothing short of disastrous. Dotty still had a way to go helping her to colour-co-ordinate her outfits — her spotty blouse and a floral skirt were a complete no-no.

Patsy was knowledgeable on so many subjects that Dotty knew little about, and Dotty always came away after one of their chats feeling liked she'd learnt something new. Today when she called in to see her, they ended up talking about the Serengeti. As Patsy rolled information off her tongue, Dotty wondered if she was related to David Attenborough.

"Wildebeest eat the short grass, while the zebras go for the long grass." Dotty nodded, taking it all in. "Did you know that the Maasai warriors wear red because they believe it wards off the lions? Also, they drink blood to alleviate hangovers."

"Well, I won't be giving that one a try." They laughed together.

Patsy agreed to take some business cards that Dotty left, and she put a poster in her window. With a little help from her business neighbours, it shouldn't be long before she picked up some customers. She also made some flyers which she delivered door-to-door. She took Winnie with her as it seemed a good idea. Winnie would get a walk and Dotty would get her deliveries done. It didn't work out that way. At one home, a lady opened the front door when she saw Dotty walking up the path and Winnie grabbed the moment and ran inside the house.

"Winnie!" Dotty gasped in horror. "I'm so sorry. She's normally so well behaved."

"Get her out, get her out!" the woman, who was scared of dogs, including small poodles, cried.

Winnie got upset with the shouting and turned suddenly in the lady's hall, knocking over a crystal vase full of flowers. Dotty flinched as the shattered glass smashed against the wooden floor. The woman screamed making Winnie panic even more.

"Get that monster out of my house," she squealed. Dotty took umbridge to Winnie being called a monster, as did Winnie who started growling, realising she had made an enemy. She grabbed the woman's skirt with its elasticated waist in her teeth and Winnie and the woman grappled together.

Within seconds, Winnie won out and the woman's skirt lay at her feet, just as her husband arrived on the scene to figure what the noise was about. Dotty had never witnessed Winnie undressing anyone before.

"What on earth are you doing, dear?" the pompous sounding husband cried.

"Get the wretched thing out of here!" The woman's face turned puce. Dotty didn't think she would gain any business from this household. After she'd agreed to pay for the cost of a replacement vase, Dotty walked home with Winnie, feeling despondent.

A hundred yards down the road and Dotty's phone rang. She hoped her luck had changed, and it was a customer. She glanced at the name on the screen, it was

Rachel. Rachel phoned to say that George should have the DNA results by the end of the week. Everyone would be on tenterhooks until then.

After ending the call, Dotty and Winnie continued their walk back home. As they approached Hans and Molly's house, Dotty stopped and peered at the shed. Part of her was dying to investigate but she felt she had done enough damage for one day. After the incident with Winnie, she didn't want to rock any boats.

That evening, her hopes were raised again as her phone rang. She looked down. It was Rachel calling for the second time. She was crying.

"Whatever is the matter, Rachel?"

"It's Marvin," she sobbed.

"What? Has he been up to his old tricks again?"

"No, nothing like that. He's had a near-death experience. I could have lost him."

"Why what's happened?"

"He was working in Horsham on one of the high-rise flats. He was cleaning the windows in the cradle. You know how unsafe those things are when it gets windy."

"Yes."

"Well someone opened their window, took out a pair of scissors and cut his cord."

"You're joking." Dotty put a hand over her mouth as she stood on the threshold of her front door.

"He was left dangling."

"So… I… presume he survived?"

"Luckily, an observer spotted him and raised the alarm. He was dragged in. It was attempted murder, Dotty."

"Gosh, why would anyone do that?"

"The police found the flat where the incident happened and interviewed the guy who did it. He has mental health issues, and he thought it was Norman Osborn."

"Who on earth is Norman Osborn?"

"The green goblin."

"Sorry, I'm not with you."

"It's Spiderman's arch enemy. The young man knew Marvin wasn't Spiderman, so assumed he must be Spiderman's enemy. Marvin had to be treated in hospital for shock. I don't think he'll go to those flats again which is a good thing because that's where you know who lives."

"What the woman he cheated with?"

"Correct."

"Well, that's karma for you. It's one way of keeping him away from her, getting someone to bump him off. I'm sorry, Rachel, you must be very upset." They ended the call and Dotty chuckled to herself. She didn't like to think bad of anyone, but that couldn't have happened to a better person, in Dotty's eyes.

Chapter 11

Dotty's marketing efforts weren't in vain as she picked up two potential customers. She hoped that at least one of her friends would join her for her first real lead. Unfortunately, they were both busy. She was nervous to deal with business matters on her own, but she had no choice. The first address she visited turned out to be a large house in Bramber overlooking the castle. It was an elderly couple who lived there. Mrs Donnington had been in the florist's shop the same afternoon that Dotty was there, and Patsy had been singing her praises. There was no way Dotty would let her know this was potentially her first proper job after the disaster at George's had gone pear-shaped. They wanted their garden tidying up and had their own sit-down mower. Dotty thought that sounded like fun. She didn't like to admit that she hadn't used one before, so got around it by saying she had never used that model before. The couple didn't mind. They both struggled with their mobility so were glad of any help.

Dotty had sent off for a book on gardening and had been going through it, page by page. If she was to make a success of this venture, she had to learn about all things horticultural. It didn't help her with the Donnington's place, but it didn't matter as she landed the job. They probably just liked her, she thought.

She went back the following day to cut their lawn. After whizzing up and down their garden trying to keep the lines straight, they offered her some home-made lemonade. She believed that was a sign that they were pleased with her work and she had a spring in her step as she made her way home.

She was about to walk up the drive to her front door when she spotted Hans next door. He stood in the window looking out at her. Dotty lowered her gaze. Her stomach churned. There was something about Hans that gave her the creeps. He was up to no good. From his facial expression, he knew she was on to him.

All that grafting in the afternoon should have whipped up a healthy appetite for Dotty, but Hans' staring eyes stunted any desire to eat and she no longer felt hungry. She went to her room and put on an old Glen Miller track. She loved listening to swing music and the big bands of that era. Her mind wandered off. She could lose herself thinking about what it must have been like in those days. Young men were more polite. They asked women to dance. Nowadays they grabbed hold of you or danced on their own. Dotty wanted someone who would treat her like a lady as in the old films. She dreamed of meeting a partner like Humphrey Bogart in Casablanca or Paul Newman in the Long, Hot Summer.

She'd not dated for a while, so romance was well overdue. Her friends swore by Tinder. Swiping right wasn't for her. Dotty wanted to be courted in the old-fashioned way and wasn't looking for a quick how's your father behind the bike sheds. The way things were going, she would be waiting a while.

The last guy she went out with, Josh, she met at a sausage manufacturing factory. She signed up through an agency to work there. Her job was packing while he worked in the processing section. She had to admit that at first, she didn't fancy him with his white coat, white hat and net on. It was when their eyes met in the locker room that the sparks started dancing in her tummy. Dotty asked him out, which wasn't what Lauren Bacall would have done, but these were desperate times. She hadn't even kissed anyone in over twelve months when she talked Josh into going ten-pin bowling with her. He blushed but accepted. Their relationship never got off the ground. He was too shy for Dotty. At first, when he spoke about sausages, she was buzzing. She thought he had the same interest in food that she had. Sadly, he was only interested in the processing of them. Sausages were a means to an end. Sausages paid the bills. He talked about the manufacturing process and the gunge that went into making them. Apart from that, his conversation comprised of discussing the pluses and minuses of a variety of video games that Dotty neither understood nor wanted to. After the third date, she had heard enough of Josh's less than riveting conversation. There was no future for them. It wouldn't last. They hadn't got further than first base, a snog and a fumble whilst watching a war film at the local cinema.

The problem was when she tried to let Josh down lightly, he wouldn't go down without a fight. The three-week relationship ended up taking nine months before he finally got the message he'd been pied. It put Dotty off the opposite sex for a while. Now that she had been single for some time, she was ready to mingle again. A night out in Brighton was called for and she hoped Kylie and Rachel would be up for it.

So long as it didn't end like last time they went down to the seaside. Kylie had been extra friendly to a guy she met on the pier and she seemed surprised when he turned up to meet her later that day. Dotty and Rachel left the love birds alone to get to know each other, but it was more than a stick of rock that Kylie came back with. Three days later, Dotty escorted a very nervous Kylie to the STI clinic, vowing never to leave her friend on her own in Brighton again.

Friday soon came around and Dotty and her two friends had arranged another extraordinary meeting over at Rachel's grandad's house. They wanted to be there when he got the DNA results. George was leaning forward in his armchair when the girls arrived. Rachel's mum, Sandra had turned up for the reveal. Everyone looked nervous as if they were in a hospital waiting room.

George clasped his hands together as though in prayer. He quietly contemplated what the results would mean. Rachel glanced over at him. His face looked tired. His brow was more furrowed than before. She could tell he hadn't been sleeping, even without asking, she knew. George's eyes continued to watch the others. His lips remained sealed. He would speak when he had to and not before.

Rachel thought about her poor grandad. It was bad enough that his wife was no longer present mentally for him. By all intents and purposes, he was on his own and he missed Mavis. He had been a devoted husband. He always did the shopping and whilst he may not have been the best with a mop or hoover, he could make a mean roast dinner. He didn't deserve this tragedy unfolding in front of him in his winter years.

There was a knock at the door.

"I'll go," Rachel said, looking at the others. No one spoke. There were sighs and tight lips. The anticipation in the room was unnerving.

Two police officers walked in, a male and a female who they had met before.

"How are you, George?" the officer asked.

"I'll be all the better after you let me out of my misery." The officer nodded.

"Please, have a seat." Sandra moved out of the way to let the police officers sit down.

"Well, George, you know the reason we are here. It is to bring you the results of our findings regarding the human remains discovered in your garden." George breathed in deeply. He let out a large gasp of air.

"Would anyone like a drink?" Sandra asked the police officers.

"No, let's get this over with." George's face tightened, and he began tapping the corner of the chair. The policeman nodded.

"That's fine. I realise you are impatient to find out the results. The facts that have come through, George, are that there is no correlation with the remains and either yours or your wife's DNA."

"Sorry, what does that mean. Speak up. I'm hard of hearing." George cupped his hand around his ear and bent his head to one side.

"It wasn't Nana's baby, Grandad." Rachel went up to her grandad's chair, knelt in front of him and took his hands in hers. "Nana is in the clear." She wiped a tear from her eye.

"So, what happens now, then?"

"Our investigations will continue. We need to find out who the mystery baby is, but in the meantime, no arrests are imminent."

"Good, I didn't think Mavis would cope very well in jail. She doesn't like porridge." For the first time in ages, George managed a smile, and the others followed suit.

Chapter 12

Dotty took Winnie for a walk the following day. They had time to digest the news the police told them. It turned out the body dated back to 1955. The good thing was, it put George in the clear for having any connection because he didn't live in the house back then. Their marital home had belonged to Mavis's parents, so Mavis would have been living there and been a young girl at the time. Her parents had long since died so that was a dead-end finding out any information that way.

When George and Mavis got married, they rented their own place in London but because they were struggling, and rents were high, they moved in with Mavis's parents. That was in the early sixties. They had lived there ever since. Mavis's father died not long after they went to stay. He had been a smoker all his life and his breathing was bad. He couldn't leave the house towards the end and needed an oxygen mask, so it was a blessing when he passed. Mavis's mother lived another ten years. It was breast cancer that took her. In those days, no one survived cancer. The wonder drug, Tamoxifen wasn't on the scene. Mercifully, Mavis's mum went quickly.

So, who did the bones belong to? Mavis's parents and Mavis would have lived at the house at the time the bones were buried. They weren't around now to throw any light on the matter. Dotty paid Audrey another visit.

She walked over to Audrey's bungalow with Winnie and was surprised to find it in darkness. Audrey hadn't mentioned going away, but it didn't look like she was home. Dotty tried the bell several times and was about to go snooping around the back when the next-door neighbour arrived on the scene.

"I haven't seen her for two days," the woman with snowy-white hair and folded arms said.

"I'm Dotty, a friend of Mavis's granddaughter. You know, Audrey's friend Mavis who is now in a home."

"Ah yes, Audrey talked about her."

"Is it unusual for Audrey not to be seen?"

"It is because she is always hanging washing out as long as it isn't raining. She does a bit at a time. I keep telling her it's best to get it over with in one fell swoop, but Audrey won't listen. She fusses around, doing bits here and there. I badger her to slow down because she's just making more work for herself. I'm Marie, by the way."

The neighbour liked to talk. She probably didn't get out much or have many visitors, Dotty thought. Finding someone to listen to her set her off like a clockwork toy. Dotty didn't think her batteries would die out anytime soon, so she interrupted.

"I'm going to go around the back to see if I can find out anything."

"Audrey wouldn't be too keen on us sneaking around. It might make her jump if she catches us out the back."

"Yes, but after what you've said, I'm concerned about her. I think I'll take a look."

Dotty ignored the neighbour's chatter. She couldn't open the back gate. It must have been bolted from inside. She dragged Audrey's wheelie bin over and climbed up. She shimmied over the fence, much to the protests of Marie. Dotty could do without her interference but once over the other side, she unlocked the gate and let Marie in.

The pair peered through Audrey's French windows. Dotty cupped her hands over her eyes and leaned against the glass. There was no sign of Audrey. They couldn't tell if she had been there recently. They were about to move away from the window when Dotty saw something.

"Wait a minute. What's that?"

"What's what, dear?"

"Can you see in the corner over the other side of the room, behind the chair? Is that a slipper poking out?

Sure enough, a tiny piece of fur pointed out around the edge of the chair.

"My eyesight isn't that brilliant, sorry. I can't tell." Dotty peered again.

"I think that might be Audrey. I'll call the police and an ambulance to be on the safe side." Dotty wouldn't listen to Marie. She made an executive decision. Now she was a businesswoman, she could do that.

While they waited for the emergency services to arrive, Dotty checked to see if there were any windows open but there weren't. She tried the doorbell and knocked a few more times. She didn't want to embarrass Audrey if she'd got it wrong.

There was no way in without smashing a window or breaking a door down. When the police arrived, they broke in through a small side window. They entered the house and Dotty and Marie followed them. Dotty had been right. Audrey lay on the floor out cold. She came to when the policewoman shook her. She looked dazed, not remembering at first what happened.

"How long have you been there?" the policewoman asked her.

Audrey looked confused. She couldn't understand what the fuss was about.

"I had a funny turn. What day is it?"

They worked out that Audrey had been on the floor since the previous afternoon. She was dehydrated which added to her confusion. She was checked over and the paramedics took her to hospital where they kept her in for a few days. They discovered that Audrey hadn't been eating properly and low blood pressure had probably caused her to collapse. Audrey's married son and daughter both travelled over to see her. They didn't live close by so were grateful to Dotty for finding their mum. They bought her a big bouquet to show their appreciation.

The outcome of the incident was that Audrey's family arranged for carers to come in twice a day to make sure Audrey was eating properly. They organised for her to have an alarm button to wear around her neck in case she fell again. Audrey was an independent lady, and she told them she wasn't ready for the knacker's yard yet.

Dotty and her friends kept in touch with Audrey. Rachel knew her nana would have wanted her to. When Audrey seemed back to her old self, Dotty had a word with her about what she'd originally intended to ask. Audrey was relieved that the body in the garden had nothing to do with Mavis or George, but Dotty pressed her for more information.

"Could there be any link with Mavis's parents and the baby, do you think?" Dotty asked.

"It's interesting that you say that because I've been racking my brains. If I remember rightly, Mavis did voluntary work at the cottage hospital in the neighbouring village when she finished school."

"Okay, can you tell me more about that?"

"The hospital is a Catholic care home these days. Back in the fifties and sixties, it was where unmarried mothers were kept."

"What do you mean by kept?" Dotty frowned.

"It was where mothers went to have their illegitimate babies. It was a mental institution."

"I don't understand." Dotty's eyes widened. "Unmarried mothers were kept in a mental institution?"

"That's correct. It happened all over the country in those days."

"That's awful. I can't believe it."

"There was a real stigma attached to having a baby out of wedlock back then. Any young girl who got pregnant brought shame on the family, so they were sent away, and they came to places like the Riverside hospital as it was known."

"It's incredible what went on. Is there anywhere I can find more information?"

"The local library might help. I don't know if anyone is still alive who worked there."

"Okay, well I'm fascinated by what you've told me, so I will see if I can research it some more."

Dotty got up to leave. She made her way to the door.

"There is one other thing," Audrey said.

"What's that then?"

"I remember that Mavis contacted the young girl who she befriended back then. I can't recall her name now." Audrey looked towards the ceiling and frowned. Dotty waited. "What the devil was her name?"

"If you think of it, can you let me know?"

"Of course, wait a minute. It was Karen, Karen, oh, what was her surname? If you hang on a minute, it will come to me. It's just been misfiled in that brain of mine." Dotty stood waiting.

"Karen Southgate, that was it."

"Thank you, Audrey. I'll look into it and see what I can find out about Karen Southgate."

Chapter 13

Saturday's meeting at the café proved to be fruitful. If the trio were to get to the bottom of this mystery, there was work to be done. Kylie volunteered to go to the library. Dotty called at the care home to see what she could learn. Rachel, the only Catholic amongst the three went to see a priest who knew the Riverside. They came together to compare notes.

"You go first, Kylie." Kylie brought out some paperwork on the notes she made. She had even taken photographs. She passed copies to the girls.

"This is very efficient, Kylie."

"If a job's worth doing, then it's worth doing well. That was what my dad always told me. Here we are. This is very interesting." The other two pulled their chairs in closer. Rachel read from a sheet she had prepared.

"The Riverside was opened in 1910 as a Catholic Inebriate Woman's Reformatory. Under the Inebriates Act of 1898, the institution was built to separate women who had problems from society. The act sent habitual drinkers away. After the First World War, they widened their intake to include what they classed as 'mental defectives.' The nurses were known as 'subnormal nurses' and in the 1950s it changed its name to 'the Hospital for the Mentally Subnormal'. Many of the women were admitted because they dared to have a child out of wedlock. They had nowhere else to go. They were abandoned by their families and the hospital took them in, even though there was nothing mentally wrong with them. The sad thing was that they lived in there for so long that they became institutionalised. It would have been criminal to let them out and expect them to survive in the wider community. When it became a care home in the nineties, over eighty women lived there.

The other two looked at her, stunned. Both because of the revelations about the unmarried women and the effect the system had on their lives.

"I always thought it was just an ordinary hospital. I never knew about this. It seems so cruel," Rachel said.

"Thank goodness it isn't like that today. I'd love to talk to someone still alive who was in there. It's important that we try to find out more about Mavis's friend, Karen Southgate," Dotty said.

"I found this statement written by the chairman of the Inebriate Board," Kylie said.

"Gosh, you have been busy." Rachel nodded to her and looked at her papers.

"When the hospital opened, the chairman expressed his heartfelt wish that all inmates who might come within the hospital's walls would be restored to happier and brighter lives. I don't think his wish came true. I read an article which described the inmates as idiots, imbeciles and feeble-minded persons. It makes me shudder to think what life must have been like there. We need to find out more. It makes fascinating reading."

"You're right." Dotty nodded. "Why did they have to use such derogatory terminology?"

"It was a sign of the times. That was how things were back then. I believe we can access archives of patient records if we pay a small fee."

"I think we should do it."

"I second that," Rachel said. "How did you get on, Dotty?"

"Not much joy, I'm afraid. No one has any details of the previous life of the building. My money is on following up on Kylie's research. What's your opinion, Rachel?"

"Good idea. I didn't get very far with my guy, either. I went to see Father Tom, and he told me in the nicest possible way to keep my nose out."

"What?" Kylie looked across at her friend, her mouth wide open.

"That's right. His opinion is to let sleeping dogs lie. He said those were different times and they wouldn't get away with any of that behaviour today, but he likened the women's treatment to Victorian schooldays. Even my parents talk about physical punishments when they were young. They were caned and had their knuckles rapped with a ruler if they got anything wrong at school." Rachel's mouth narrowed.

"It doesn't bear thinking about, does it? No wonder our parents tell us we don't know how lucky we are and that we have things too cushy these days. It seems they are right." Dotty folded her arms and looked up, taking in all that she had heard.

The girls made plans to do further research. Kylie enjoyed going to the library and she could fit it in around her shifts at the pub.

"I'll go back and see Audrey. Her memory is great, given how old she is. She might remember other names of people from that time who still live in the area that we can ask," Dotty said.

"That's great, and I'll talk to Grandad George. He could have some knowledge of the hospital. It may not be connected to Dotty's discovery, but it makes interesting reading if nothing else."

Dotty walked home after saying goodbye to her friends. She thought about their plans for the following week. The others were coming over to her house on Friday for a pampering evening. She would get some products in — face packs, creams, and two bottles of Prosecco. It was easier to put the world to rights after a glass or two of bubbly. The girls knew how to party. It didn't matter that it was just three of them. Thank goodness the Inebriates Act wasn't still in force today. She often got sozzled at weekends. It made living in a dull village so much more interesting. Plus, after a few drinks, tongues got looser. Dotty found out the gossip, even when the others had been sworn to secrecy.

She discovered plenty about the goings-on that way. Catherine Carmichael was two-timing her long-term partner and Josephine Brompton's children all had different fathers. No, the only problem with their Prosecco parties was the hangovers the following day. Every time she overdid it, Dotty said: "never again." Whenever Kylie and Rachel turned up again with Prosecco, she soon forgot how bad those headaches were.

As she neared her house, she looked up at Hans and Molly's place. The bedroom curtains were drawn. She frowned. That was unusual in the daytime. Suddenly, she noticed a silhouette of a person against the flimsy curtain material. It stopped her in her tracks. She couldn't take her eyes off the upstairs window. The actions she saw caused her to rub her eyes. Surely, this couldn't be happening. She could make out a man's figure. He was holding a whip. Not only that, he was using it. Dotty continued to gaze up. The bedroom window was open. She could just about hear a woman's voice coming from within.

"More, lover boy, more."

Dotty turned her back on the sight. Her cheeks glowed. She held her hand over her mouth, then kept turning around for a peek. When it sunk in what was going on, she sniggered. She couldn't believe Molly would be into S&M. She was too prim and proper. Mind you, it was true what they say, that it's the quiet ones you need to watch. Even though Dotty realised she wasn't far removed from being a peeping tom, she couldn't prise herself away from underneath the window. Out of the periphery of her vision, she noticed a figure turned the corner at the end of the road. As the person walked towards her, Dotty coughed and bent down to tie her already tied shoelace. She didn't want anyone suspecting that she may be a secret voyeur.

As Dotty returned to a standing position, the figure walked closer. It was a woman carrying a shopping bag. Dotty looked up in horror as she realised it wasn't just any woman walking towards her, it was Molly.

So, if Molly was out here in the road, it didn't take much detecting to work out who was in her bedroom — Greta, the whore. At least, that was what Dotty and her friends nicknamed her. She may not charge for her services, but from the look of her, if she didn't, then they thought she ought to.

Whilst Dotty had no loyalty towards Hans, she worried about the effect the sight would have on Molly if she caught her husband in a compromising position. So, Dotty tried to detain her for as long as she could. They discussed the weather, the body in the garden, the current economic climate, the Royal baby and just about everything that came into Dotty's head. Poor Molly looked exasperated when she finally got away from Dotty.

Desperate to save her blushes, Dotty tried one last time as Molly reached her front door.

"I've got a fabulous recipe for sausage and mash if ever you want to borrow it, Molly." Molly smiled and opened her front door. Dotty could have kicked herself for her last comment. Who on earth needed a recipe for sausage and mash? It was easy to make. No wonder Molly gave her a funny look. I bet she thinks I've lost the plot, Dotty thought. She listened out for any crashing sounds or altercations coming from Hans and Molly's house. When there were none, Dotty went in her own home, shaking her head. Maybe, Greta was hiding in the wardrobe.

Chapter 14

The news about Hans' sex life spread like wildfire. Normally, the three girls only gossiped amongst themselves, but this wasn't the sort of information that was easy to keep in.

As Dotty told her hairdresser, "It's not every day you find you're living next door to a kinky sex perv." Poor Hans must have wondered what the nudging and winking were about when he called in the supermarket and the local pub. Rachel decided it was a good thing that the local community had turned their attentions onto Hans. If they were talking about him, then at least they weren't discussing her grandparent's back garden and what else may be hidden below the surface. The police were convinced the garden was clear, but people still talked and speculated. It was as though they wanted the notoriety of another 10 Rillington Place on their doorstep. Mrs Bradbury at number twenty-three started having her hair done twice a week. She also put on a dusting of face powder and lipstick every day in case she got stopped in the street to give an interview.

The following week, Grace from across the road invited the local women to a lingerie party. Susie the regional top seller for May was showing the latest range of underwear to everyone. There was no obligation to buy. There never was at these things. The women felt compelled to support the hostess though, so came away with a pair of knickers, at least. However, the cheapest pair was a tenner.

"A tenner for a pair of undies," Kylie whispered to Dotty. Susie, with her keen hearing, overheard.

"Yes, but, feel the quality. You can smell the luxury." There was no way Kylie was smelling knickers for anyone. Each item was passed between the guests who seemed more interested in devouring the wine and canapes than looking at undergarments. Most of them were bored with proceedings. Kylie thought Susie should have brought in some Anne Summers sex toys to liven up the show. Susie was oblivious to the apathy. She was busy pointing out the better points of a camisole to one lady who it was wasted on. Quite honestly, she didn't know the difference between Agent Provocateur and Asda's bargain-basement range.

"My Jack would love me in these," said one large lady who held up a pair of black suspenders. Dotty and Kylie raised their eyebrows. Dotty thought it was a shame that Rachel couldn't be there. She may have found something to whet Marvin's appetite and stop him straying. On second thoughts, that was unlikely and would be a waste of money. He would have a roving eye whatever Rachel wore. Talking of which, she looked up. A few heads turned as a latecomer stood in the doorway.

"Molly, how good to see you. I'm so glad you could make it." Grace went up to Molly, kissed her cheek and shoved a glass of white wine in her hand. She hadn't noticed the nudging and whispers rippling around the room.

"I'm sorry I'm late. I had to wait until Hans got home to keep an eye on the kids."

"Yes, I understand. How are things with you and Hans?" All eyes turned to wait for Molly's reply. She smiled, not having a clue about the significance of the question.

"He's been working late a lot lately, but other than that everything is fine." The women looked at each other and nodded.

"Good, good," Grace said. She patted Molly's arm then turned to talk to someone else. The elephant filled the room, but it didn't look like anyone would say anything about Hans' recent behaviour. Molly would be kept in blissful ignorance a little while longer. Even though Dotty had seen more than anyone else regarding Hans' dallying, she didn't think it was her responsibility to put Molly in the picture. When Molly bought nothing, Dotty took that as a sign that her marriage really was on the rocks.

A few women asked for an update on the body in the garden. Dotty and Kylie were pleased to relay back the fact that Rachel's grandparents were in the clear. They knew how rumours got out of hand and became twisted. They were glad to quash any doubts.

"How's your new business venture going?" Grace asked her as Dotty handed out her business cards. She could see that having a network of local women together was a golden opportunity to gain more business.

"It's going very well, thank you."

"Finding a dead body didn't upset the apple cart then?"

"Anything but. It gave me extra publicity, so enquiries have been flooding in." Dotty didn't like to tell lies. She saw this as exaggerating the truth which wasn't the same thing. She had received two enquiries so far. Something had come of one of them. Still, it was early days. Setting up a new business took time.

By the end of the evening, the girls had helped finish the Prosecco. They felt more than a bit merry and were glad they didn't have far to walk home. They nodded at Gordon Webster who was walking his Jack

Russell. As they staggered down the road, Dotty turned to her friend.

"I loved you in that pink bra." She hiccupped.

"Well, I preferred you in those red knickers." Both girls laughed, and Gordon Webster raised his eyebrows.

Chapter 15

Something was paying off because Dotty received three more enquiries for her gardening services the following week. It called for another flick through the gardening manual. She read the section on carrots. Everything you needed to know was in that book. She rehearsed in front of the mirror what to say at the next property.

"Have you ever thought of growing your own vegetables? It's so on-trend now. Carrots grow well. We should plant them in the spring, after the last of the frost. They take seventy to eighty days to mature. There's nothing nicer than homegrown Chanterelle carrots to go with your Sunday lunch. Provided you keep rabbits away, you should get a good crop." The fact that Dotty had never grown a carrot in her life was beside the point. You had to start somewhere.

When the girls met up again on Saturday, Dotty felt guilty that she had done nothing to help move the case forward. She wasn't the only one. Kylie hadn't been to the library this week either.

"I've got an idea," said Rachel.

"Oh dear, mind your backs, brainwaves coming through," laughed Kylie holding her arms out wide.

"What is it?" Dotty asked.

"You know I've been going to church the last couple of weeks to see if any of the old folk remember anything about the Riverside?

"Yes, I'm very proud of you finding your faith again," Kylie said.

"I'm only doing it for research."

"I'm sure God won't mind and will be glad you've returned to his fold," Kylie said. Rachel scowled at her.

"Well, what I was thinking is, why don't you guys come with me? We could speak to more people if the three of us attend."

"Oh, wait a minute." Kylie put her palm facing towards Rachel. "I know I've behaved myself for the last three weeks but going to church is a bit extreme."

Never one to miss a clue, Dotty asked, "Why, what did you do three weeks ago?"

"Never you mind," Kylie blushed.

"Come on, Kylie, spit it out. Who were you humping this time?"

"I had to have some distraction after that awful incident in Brighton."

"You mean with that guy who gave you a dose and you can't even remember his name now."

"Ssh," Kylie said, coughing and almost choking on her carrot cake. She was on a health kick this week, so all her cakes had fruit or veg in them. "I bumped into Barry Barlow when I was out shopping, and we had a bit of catching up to do."

"Is that the new name for it, catching up?" Dotty laughed.

"Ugh, not Barry Barlow. You said you wouldn't go near him with a bargepole after he was seen with his tongue down Sandie Thornton's throat." Rachel pulled a face.

"When you've got a fluttering fanny, you forget about things like that. Thinking about it, a few Hail Mary's might be what I need to cleanse my mind."

"It'll take more than a few Hail Mary's to sort you out." Rachel laughed.

The upshot of their meeting was that the girls agreed to go to church the following day. They planned to speak to anyone over seventy, to see if they knew anything about the Riverside.

"So, I'm not likely to cop off at your church then, Rachel?" Kylie asked.

"I doubt it," Rachel replied.

"Okay, well I won't bother putting on my false lashes then. You should bring Marvin. It might do his conscience good to listen to a sermon on how to stop sinning."

"I doubt it. He'd probably be like the Catholic boys who come along to confession. They tell father how they have sinned and think if the slate's wiped clean, they can do it again.

The following day, Dotty made an effort and wore her best dress. It was a vintage fifties style pale green ditsy number with a wrap-around waist and a white broderie anglaise trim. She wore dainty white lace gloves and took along her straw handbag. She didn't know if the old dears would appreciate the effort she put in as she removed the rollers from her shiny auburn hair. Older people often passed comment that she looked like Rita Hayworth, so she didn't want to disappoint, and she enjoyed keeping up the Hollywood persona. To crown it off, she put on her sunglasses and floppy sunhat.

When Rachel saw her, she wondered what the priest would make of her attire, but he would probably just be happy that she had come to church.

Apart from Kylie almost falling asleep during the sermon, the service passed without incident. Dotty didn't hear much of the priest's talk either. She had been too busy admiring the stain glass windows. They sent her off into a daydream about making mosaics. She loved doing any kind of craftwork and her bedroom was filled with boxes of equipment she had bought for various projects, from card-making to sewing. She had tried her hand at ceramic painting, candle-making and jewellery and she enjoyed them all. Maybe one day she might open a shop and sell her wares. It sounded much more fun than gardening.

Rachel breathed in the scent of incense and Dotty sneezed. She took out a tissue and dabbed her nose looking for all the world like a movie star from bygone days. Rachel glanced at her friends. Where Dotty had gone over the top with her efforts, Kylie had gone to the other extreme and wore her faded jeans. She didn't care who she impressed. She'd not put on any makeup. If there were no handsome men to impress, then why should she bother.

At the end of the service, the girls moved to the back of the building. They joined the rest of the congregation to chat over a cup of coffee. The friends took time to mingle and Dotty worked the floor with poise and elegance. However, it was Kylie who came away with the best lead. She kept herself busy, scurrying around the room.

"Hello, dear. I've not seen you here before." A petite lady with snow-white hair spoke to Kylie.

"No, my parents couldn't afford to bring me. They kept me away after an incident when I was a toddler."

"Why? What happened?"

"My mother was outside the church after the service talking to the vicar. She had given me her handbag to play with and I kept circling the church and waving each time I walked past. It wasn't until we came to leave that she realised what I'd been doing. Every time I'd reached the entrance, I'd taken some money out of my mother's purse and put it in the collection box. By the time I'd finished, there was no money left in her purse. When my mother discovered what I had done, she was horrified. She could hardly ask for it back. I'm sure I was responsible for the church getting their new roof sooner than they expected that year, thanks to them having my mother's housekeeping money."

"Oh, you're funny." Kylie moved on to chat to someone else. She met a couple who had been coming to the church for twenty-four years.

"That would be around the time I went to my first christening. I made a spectacle of myself, according to my parents."

"Why, what did you do?"

"While everyone chatted in the back room, I toddled off to look at the buffet food laid out in the front room. Apparently, there was a huge bowl of trifle on display. Instead of helping myself and eating some, I devoured it in a different way."

"What happened?"

"I took my shoes and socks off and went for a paddle in it. I don't think we were invited to that house again." The couple laughed, and Kylie moved on to someone else. The third lady she spoke to, was the interesting one as she knew a nurse who had worked at the hospital back in the day. Kylie took the details and arranged to make contact.

As the girls got ready to leave the church, Father Tom approached them, his robe wafted against the table. He smiled and clasped his hands together in front of his chest, as though in prayer.

"I hope you ladies will come and visit us again."

"Thank you for the service, father. I'm sure we will."

"Rachel, tell your mother I was asking after her."

"I will, father."

"Oh, and there's just one other thing," he said pointing his finger in the air.

"What's that?" Rachel asked.

"I hear you've been asking questions about the Riverside?"

"That's correct. We're doing some research on it."

"Leave well alone. No good will come out of raking up the past. You may open a can of worms that can't be put back. It could be disastrous for everyone. The community could suffer. My advice is to stay well away."

Chapter 16

"I don't know about you guys, but if someone tells me not to do something, I do it even more. If Mum gets in the car with me and says I should slow down, I put my foot on the accelerator. It's disconcerting, people telling us not to get involved in this case. It gets my back up. All this negativity and reluctance to speak about the Riverside makes me suspicious." Dotty was busy multi-tasking, scrolling through her emails and filing her nails as she spoke.

"You're right. What we've found out so far is unpleasant to listen to. However, there could be more. I, for one, won't be stopping looking into it." Rachel looked over at her friend.

"Neither will I." Kylie piped up.

"Same here. We're like the three musketeers on a crusade. Look, guys, I've had an email from someone who used to work at the Riverside." Dotty's shoulders bounced up and down.

Father Tom's warning only caused the girls to up the stakes on their efforts. Through appeals on social media and talking to people in the village, Dotty was now in receipt of the name of a nun, Sybil Flanagan who worked at the Riverside. She lived with her sister in a small cottage just outside Pulborough. Dotty wasted no time replying. She arranged to visit Sybil the following evening.

The backdrop to Sybil's home was the River Arun and Dotty stopped for a moment to admire the view across the Brooks towards the South Downs National Park. When Dotty entered the tiny abode, she knew that something was amiss. Had they forgotten she was coming? She could smell fish and chips cooking.

"Did I get the time wrong?" she asked.

"No, we're awfully sorry. We had a power cut earlier so we've not been able to have our evening meal yet. Do you mind waiting until we've finished?" The woman who answered the door was tiny, with short grey hair. Her pale complexion did nothing to enhance her features. She wore a burgundy-coloured jumper with a black tweed skirt and black brogues on her feet.

"No, not at all." Dotty's stomach rumbled. Their meal smelled so good. She hadn't eaten, and she was famished. She sat on the sofa and was about to flick through a copy of Franciscan Spirit, a Catholic magazine, when Sybil popped her head around the door.

"There's enough food for three if you'd like to join us?"

"No, I couldn't, honestly."

"Please, it's no trouble and it would be a shame for the fish to go to waste. It was fresh off the fishmonger's today."

"Okay, if you insist."

Dotty joined them in the back room and while Sybil went to get the food and extra place settings, Harriet grinned at her. Dotty wondered if she had ever attended the Riverside as a patient. The two older women clasped their hands together.

"For what we are about to receive, may the Lord make us truly grateful, amen."

"Shall I tell Dotty about the time I got a fishbone stuck?" Harriet asked her sister.

"Dotty doesn't want to know about that." The reply didn't deter Harriet.

"I bet you think I got a fishbone stuck in my throat, don't you Dotty?" Harriet said.

"I...." Dotty looked across at Sybil and shrugged her shoulders.

"It wasn't like that. We'd just been eating fish and chips and I must have swallowed a bone. I didn't even feel it scratching at my throat or anything." Dotty started to take extra care chewing her fish as she listened.

"That's enough, Harriet. Dotty doesn't want to hear your tales of woe. It will put her off her meal." It was too late. Harriet's story had already done that.

"Well, I passed out. I was taken to hospital, and they found a fishbone that size inside me." She actioned the size of a small knife. Dotty's eyes widened. Harriet bent forward towards Dotty.

"I'm lucky to be alive." Dotty was about to swallow a piece of fish, but it lodged in her throat through fear of choking. It refused to go down until Dotty chewed it so much her jaw ached.

"Harriet, that's enough. Dotty doesn't want to hear this." Sybil turned to Dotty. "I must apologise for my sister. She tells that story every time we have visitors. It's just a shame you were also eating fish. I understand if Harriet has put you off and you don't want to eat anymore." Dotty left the rest of the fish. Harriet's tale had affected her appetite. She tried to hide the last portion underneath a few chips.

When they finished the meal, Dotty glanced over at the upright piano in the corner.

"Oh wonderful, you've got a piano. Do you both play?"

"Neither of us are very good. How about you? Are you a musician?" Sybil asked.

"I don't play much anymore, but I was musical at school. After learning the recorder, I took up the piano, then the violin and flute. Nowadays, I just play the guitar."

"Good for you. It's wonderful when God gives us musical talents." Harriet smiled and clapped her hands together. "Play for us now."

"Oh, I couldn't. I'm not that good. We got rid of our piano to make room for the new sofa. I'm very rusty."

"Please, please, play for us. You can't let your gift go to waste." Dotty couldn't resist. She was itching to tinkle the ivories.

"Do you have any music?" Harriet pulled the top off the piano stool.

"We only have hymns. Will they do?"

"I suppose I can have a go."

Within minutes, Dotty belted out a rendition of "All things bright and beautiful" with the three of them joining in the singing. Dotty thought what her friends would think if they could see her now. It was a bit different to her singing a Stormzy song as she did her ironing. After Dotty completed a medley of hymns, Harriet went to make tea and they sat down to drink and eat. As soon as Dotty mentioned the word Riverside, the atmosphere changed. She tucked into a slice of lemon drizzle cake and wondered how to proceed. She waited for the probable rebuff.

"You've got to understand that back then it was different to today. I've made my peace with my maker and I can't do any more than that," Sybil said.

"What can you tell me about working there?" Sybil looked at her sister who frowned and turned away. She wouldn't get any support from her sibling. Dotty watched the wrinkle lines on Sybil's face deepen.

"Loyalty has always been something that is an important quality to me." Dotty nodded. Sybil cleared her throat. "We weren't sworn to secrecy, but confidentiality was and still is a key concept for the medical profession. Some girls had tough upbringings. They came from broken homes. Divorce was virtually unheard of. Many of the girls had no moral fibre and often they didn't know the difference between right and wrong."

"You don't have to tell me about specific cases. I would like to get a general feel for how the place was run and what went on."

"Yes, of course. We tried to educate the girls. Some were completely mad. Others could be violent. It was a lot different working there than when I spent my early years in a nunnery. It broadened my outlook."

"You'd have seen more of what life was really like." Dotty threw her a smile, but Sybil didn't return it.

The landline phone rang. It was on a small trestle table, the other side of the room. Sybil went over to answer it.

"Good evening, Father Tom. Yes, she's here now. We've just eaten. I see. Yes, yes, of course." Sybil glanced over at Dotty, a strange expression crossed her face. "Very well, I can do that. Goodnight father Tom."

Any warmth that Sybil had shown towards Dotty disappeared after the phone call. She went frosty. Dotty assumed correctly that she wouldn't get any more information out of her.

"Father Tom sends his regards." Dotty nodded. She wondered what else father Tom had said. "I'm sorry, Dotty. It's been lovely to meet you, but Harriet and I are both tired. It's one of the unfortunate side effects of getting old. We sleep a lot."

"Oh no, is it bedtime, Sybil?" Harriet asked looking at a non-existent watch on her wrist and then over at her sister.

"It's nearly that time. We must see our guest out." Sybil smiled. There was nothing more Dotty could do here. She doubted she'd get anything more out of the sisters either now or in the future.

Chapter 17

Rachel cycled over to Grandad George's after she finished work. It was a pleasant evening and the exercise would do her good. If she needed to pick up any shopping for him, she could pop it in the basket at the front. She hoped he didn't want a crate of Guinness or anything cumbersome like that.

He didn't need much, so Rachel could manage the shopping and balance her bike. George was one of those old-fashioned souls who still had milk delivered from the milkman. Well, it was the local farm, actually, and they delivered most of George's groceries — eggs, bread, cheese, fruit and veg. They'd been delivering for years. When they heard about George's unfortunate discovery in the garden, Nelly, the farmer's wife, put in an extra cherry pie that she'd baked, to cheer George up. He was over the moon and even though it was three weeks since that act of kindness, he spoke about it to everyone he encountered.

"Wasn't that nice of Nelly to bake me a cherry pie? I can taste it now. It was yummy," he said when Rachel arrived with his groceries.

"I'd have bought you a cherry pie if you'd asked."

"Oh no, I don't want one. It's no good for my waistline," George said, patting his stomach and breathing in. His liking for the odd glass of beer or two meant he displayed a more than ample beer belly. After tidying around the house, Rachel sat down with her grandad and a cup of coffee.

"How are you feeling, Grandad, now that everything has died down with the skeleton we found?"

"I'm still as baffled as anyone by it. I can't imagine how it got there." Rachel nodded. She looked outside.

Birds flew over and landed on the bird table. Another one arrived and started devouring the nuts and seeds that George put out.

"Did Nana talk about the time she worked at the Riverside?" George followed her gaze and watched as a squirrel tried to get in on the act.

"She didn't say much. It affected her though. I always thought there was a sadness about her when she mentioned it."

"In what way?"

"She wouldn't say a lot, but she lost her happy-go-lucky side when she spoke about the place. Her mood changed. She said it made her appreciate what she had. Some of those girls had a rough time."

"I believe after talking to Audrey that she befriended one of the girls."

"Do you think that body is anything to do with her?"

"I don't know, Grandad. Can you remember what happened to her? I've been told her name was Karen. Did Nana ever talk about her?"

"Not much."

"Did Karen have any family?"

"She had a brother who lived in London somewhere. Sorry, I can't be much help. It was a long time ago." Rachel nodded.

"That's okay, Grandad. I understand." They finished their drinks and Rachel left her grandad with his memories and said goodbye.

Next, it was Dotty and Kylie's turn to get busy. The lady who Kylie was in touch with from the church said her father worked as a nurse at the hospital in the fifties and sixties. Kylie mistakenly thought the nurse was a woman. Kylie spoke to the daughter over the phone. She said that her father, Norman came over from Mauritius in the late fifties.

The girls were excited to visit him and hoped he could provide them with more information about the Riverside. He lived in a flat in a retirement complex close by, so they went to see him.

His movements were slow. He had forgotten what it felt like to have joints that moved freely, pain-free. His aches were now his constant companion. The dark complexion brought out his bone structure and with his bald head and thin frame, he reminded Dotty of Gandhi. She watched his hand movement as he expressed himself, slow and purposeful. Liver spots were still prominent through his dark skin. His long bony talons looked like a bird's claws. He smiled as he spoke. His memories warmed and haunted him, but he seemed happy to talk.

"I arrived from Mauritius back in 1959 to train as a subnormal nurse, as they were called then. I was only nineteen and very frightened. It was a long journey, coming all that way on my own. I can still remember my first day. It was so exciting. I was taken to my room in the nurse's home and given an apple to eat. I can recall how nice the building smelt. The whole place seemed so magical. I have plenty to be thankful for. Working there gave me a wonderful life. I met my wife, Patience there. She was a nurse as well. Sadly, she passed away last year."

"So, they were happy memories you had of your job there?" Dotty asked.

"Very. I loved working with those talented people. My favourite occasion was in the early sixties when a then-unknown pop group came to entertain the patients one Christmas. You may have heard of them. They were called the Beatles." Everyone laughed. Norman had thrown a different light on his time at the hospital than others had mentioned.

"Did anything happen there that you weren't happy about?" Kylie asked. The room went silent. The girls waited for Norman to answer. He thought for some time.

"The saddest part was how the patients were dealt with by outsiders. Children especially would come up to the railings and shout out cruel names. They threw rotten fruit over the fence. The Riverside community were treated as outcasts by local people. It was no wonder they struggled to integrate back into society when the place closed. That was my worst nightmare. I cried like a baby when it shut its doors for the last time. It had given me so much, you see. Thanks to my job there, I was able to have a home and a family, very precious things to me."

"I heard children were born there. Is that correct?" Dotty asked.

"Yes, some of them became institutionalised. They didn't find out what life was like in the outside world until the place closed. It was criminal how they were cast aside. Many of them couldn't cope."

"What happened to them?"

"They were housed in supported living accommodation, so physically they were looked after but mentally it was a disgrace. Many didn't know how to survive on their own."

"That sounds very sad." Dotty glanced across at Norman who had closed his eyes.

"I still pray for them every day. Life can be so cruel sometimes."

The girls formed a picture of what life was like at the Riverside. They discussed it when they regrouped at the tea rooms the following day.

Dotty resisted the desserts and plumped instead for a salmon salad.

"Be careful eating that," Kylie said.

"Why?" Dotty frowned.

"Your halo will slip and fall on your head. It might knock you out." Kylie laughed and moved her arm away just before Dotty punched it.

"Seriously, how's the diet going, Dotty?" Kylie asked.

"It's moving forward at a snail's pace. I've lost three kilograms in total so far, so I can't grumble. At least the scales are aiming in the right direction. I'd prefer it to be more, but they say it's better if it comes off slowly."

"Don't you believe it. Mine's coming off too slowly, a tenth of a kilo a month. I'll get to my goal weight by the time I'm ninety at this rate," Kylie said. "I'm being good today. Have you noticed? I'm only having a cupcake."

"How is having a cupcake being good?" Dotty asked.

"It's lemon, so I'm getting a fifth of my fruit and veg quota for the day."

"I don't think it works like that."

"The problem I have is when I'm working. Doing physical work makes me hungry. I need a packet of crisps or a bag of nuts. I can't stop myself and always give in to temptation." Dotty wanted to question how Kylie thought pulling pints was physical work. It was nothing next to her exertions in the garden, but she kept her thoughts to herself.

"Talking of temptation, are things quiet on the fella front?" Rachel asked.

"Yes, I've been celibate for at least a fortnight, but we've got our trip to Brighton coming up next week girls, so hold your horses." They laughed.

"That's handy because there's a new name come forward. I've found someone who was in the Riverside as a patient and she lives just outside Brighton. We could visit her before our night out."

"Sounds like a plan. What's her name?"

"Florence McMurray."

"Well Florence, I wonder if you will have anything interesting to tell us about the Riverside?" Kylie spoke to the painting on the wall. The girls looked at each other and raised their eyebrows.

"The plot thickens." Dotty raised her eyebrows.

Chapter 18

Rachel was secretly looking forward to their night out more than the other two. She told herself that if the right guy came along, she would kick Marvin into touch. She didn't want to do it the other way around. Being single abhorred her. It might be okay for her friends, but she liked to have a man about the place.

They got the train to Brighton. It wasn't a good idea to take a car. It cost an arm and a leg to park. Plus, it meant they could have a few drinks. Provided they didn't overdo things, they could get the last train home and then a taxi from the station. They had to catch a bus to just outside Worthing to Florence's address. They wondered how she would cope with the three of them descending en masse, but she told Dotty there was no problem with them turning up.

She lived in a small terraced house, a few streets away from the seafront. The seagulls squawked so loud it was deafening. The girls knocked on Florence's front door. A tiny frail woman with thinning white hair opened it. She bit her lip and her eyes darted around. She wore a thin light-blue cotton dress and a large handmade cardigan that had holes in the elbows. When the girls introduced themselves, Florence's high-pitched laugh sounded more nervous than genuine.

Dotty gave her a huge smile. She wanted to reassure her they weren't there to rob her but by the looks of things she had nothing worth pinching. The brown sofa was shabby and worn. Cat marks had frayed the material. She had a small two-bar electric fire that looked like it was ready for throwing on the tip. Her carpet was threadbare, and the wallpaper was dated. The whole place looked in need of a lick of paint.

"I wanted to put your mind at ease, Florence. We are here to research the Riverside." Dotty explained about the discovery and her hunch that the body may be connected to the old hospital. "Could you to tell us about your time there?"

"I managed to escape." Florence avoided eye contact.

"Escape? Really?" Kylie said. "What happened?"

"I was working in the canteen. I'd gone outside for a smoke. A van brought a delivery of food, so the gates were open. There was no one about so I took my chance and legged it."

"So, are you saying you were a prisoner there?"

Florence sighed. She bit the skin off the side of her thumb.

"I got pregnant when I was seventeen. The baby's father was in the navy and he scarpered. I never saw him after I told him I was expecting. My parents insisted that I had the baby. They were both from a strong Irish Catholic upbringing. Two men came in white coats and took me away. They took me to the Riverside. It was a horrible place. I'll never forget all those poor women in the same boat as me. There was always an air of sadness hanging over us. None of those women wanted to give up their babies, but they were forced to. I had to have my son adopted, and I never saw him again." Florence wiped a tear from her eye. The girls watched her, listening in stunned silence.

"There were women with mental health issues. They screamed and behaved strangely. It was scary. I felt abandoned by my family. Nobody cared what became of me."

"So, what happened when you broke free? Where did you go?"

"I hitchhiked to London. I lived on the streets for a time until a charity took me in. They were tough times. I changed my name because I was scared of them finding me and putting me back in the hospital."

"So, let me get this straight. You were in a mental institution and the only thing wrong with you was that you were an unmarried mother?" Rachel frowned.

"A childless unmarried mother." She nodded. Kylie and Dotty sat there with mouths agog.

"Were all the children put up for adoption?"

"No, some lived there but my family insisted I gave my child up. I never forgave them for that."

"Did your son ever try to find you?"

"Not as far as I know. I didn't make things easy because I changed my name."

"How very sad."

"Do you remember any of the others?"

"I don't want to get into trouble. I'd rather not say if you don't mind. They might not want it divulging. It wasn't a nice place. I was deeply ashamed to be there, so it isn't something that many women would admit to."

"We understand." There was little else the girls could ask Florence if she wouldn't provide them with any more information. They thanked her and were about to leave.

"From what you've told me, do you think the baby's remains you found were linked to someone at the Riverside?"

"It's possible," Dotty nodded.

"Good luck with that. Don't be surprised if you find more than you expect."

They weren't sure what she meant but visiting Florence had affected them. They were subdued as they travelled back to Brighton.

"Well, guys, I need a drink after that," said Kylie. "What a sad life, poor Florence."

"We don't appreciate how fortunate we are being born today, what with the pill and the way attitudes have changed." Dotty ordered a bottle of Prosecco. They chatted together for some time. They even got propositioned by a drunk. However, none of the girls got lucky that night. The men seemed focused on getting drunk and making fools of themselves.

"It's so unattractive, seeing grown men acting like five-year-olds." Kylie's words were slurred. She wobbled towards the exit of the wine bar. Then she tried to climb a lamppost. She was more than slightly merry. They settled for a kebab on the way home. Florence's tale had put them off men.

The following day, Dotty took Winnie for a walk. Her head throbbed, and she wished she'd not had that last glass of bubbly. Suddenly, she spotted Hans with Greta walking a few hundred yards in front of her. She followed them and when they turned up towards Hans' driveway, she waited to see where they went. They disappeared into the shed again. That probably meant that Molly must be in the house. What a cheek, she thought.

Feeling brave, she tiptoed up the path and got within a few feet of the shed when disaster struck. Winnie saw a cat and started barking. Afraid of being found out, Dotty dived behind a bush in the garden.

Hans opened the shed door.

"Who's there?" he cried out.

Dotty was having palpitations. Sadly, Winnie hadn't joined her behind the bush and was busy wrestling with a paper bag. She knew Hans would recognise Winnie, so she couldn't stay hidden. She crept out from behind the bush on all fours. Hans watched as she stood up, her shoulders slumped and her hair full of twigs and leaves.

"What the blazes are you doing here?"

"I... I... was looking for Winnie," she said sheepishly as she brushed herself down. Hans' eyes narrowed.

Both Greta and Molly heard the commotion and arrived on the scene.

"What are you doing in our garden?" Molly asked, her arms on her hips.

"Can't you see, your husband is having an affair." Dotty blurted out, pointing at Hans. Greta poked her head from behind him. She held a sheet of paper in her hand.

"What is all this nonsense about?" Hans said.

"You can't deny it. I've heard you at it and seen you in the bedroom with your whip." The other three started laughing. "What's so funny?" Dotty frowned. "What's the joke."

"Hans and Greta are both in the next production of *A Steamy Romance*. It's a farcical play run by the amateur dramatic society. I'm sure he would be happy to sell you a ticket to watch him," Molly said.

"Oh, I see." Dotty didn't know where to look. She felt so stupid. "Winnie," she cried out with a quiver in her voice as Winnie had disappeared. "Winnie, are you there?" Winnie padded up, wagging her tail and Dotty turned and marched down the drive. She would have to apologise to Hans and Greta. Not yet though, she was too embarrassed right now.

Chapter 19

On Wednesday evening, Dotty was getting ready for bed. She had just cleaned her teeth and brushed her hair with a hundred strokes. That was a ritual her auntie Mo had taught her. It was supposed to make her hair glossy and strong. Dotty wasn't sure if it worked because there was so much hair on the brush when she finished. When Dotty questioned her auntie about that, Mo said that was dead hair anyway that needed replenishing to make way for the new growth. It wasn't often that Dotty got to one hundred. She usually lost count but tonight she had a good go at it.

She hoped that looking good would boost her confidence and that she wouldn't feel as dumb. After all, she had started what she now knew to be a rumour about Hans. She had to put it right somehow. She would do what she could to make herself look less like a clown and more like a local businesswoman who could be taken seriously.

Dotty's phone rang. It was Kylie. Dotty frowned. It was unusual to get a call from any of her friends so late. A text maybe, but not a call.

"Hi, Kylie, what's up?" Dotty sensed the excitement in Kylie's voice.

"You'll never guess what."

"What?"

"I've been working at the Six Bells tonight as you know, and it was quiet. Graham doesn't like me doing nothing, so I polished the glasses. Then when I'd finished that I perched myself at the end of the bar talking to two of the punters."

"Go on."

"I told them about our research, and they sounded interested so I mentioned that we were searching to find anything we could about Karen Southgate. Well, would you believe it, one of the guys, Mike only knows her brother, David. I couldn't believe my luck. What do you think of that?"

"Amazing. So, did you get David's number?"

"Yes, it's too late to ring him now but I'll try to contact him tomorrow and we can take it from there."

"Good work, trouper, you deserve a bonus for this." Kylie laughed.

"You can buy me an extra cream cake on Saturday."

Dotty couldn't sleep that night as she churned over everything that they had found out so far about the Riverside. She thought of the questions they wanted to ask David and if he would tell them where his sister was. They would have to play it carefully how they approached him. If her hunch were right, it could be Karen's baby buried in George and Mavis's garden.

Kylie spoke to David the next day. He lived in Croydon now and she arranged to meet up with him the following afternoon. Rachel wasn't free to join them, but Dotty had no work so could tag along.

David met them at a cafe in town. He said it would kill two birds with one stone as he had to go shopping for a few bits. It was a nice day, so the girls sat at a table outside Pret where the rendezvous had been arranged.

They guessed it was David as soon as he started walking towards them. He had a fringe of white hair around his balding scalp. His face was wizened, and his back slightly hunched. He ambled along, unsteady on his feet. They smiled at him and when he smiled back, they knew they had found their man.

Dotty bought him a drink and a sandwich and even though he insisted on paying, she wouldn't take his money. The girls were grateful that he took the time to speak to them. Dotty returned to their table with a tray of food and drinks. She glanced across at David. His eyes danced around. He had one of those faces that looked lived in. The map of wrinkles on his face must have wondrous stories to tell, Dotty thought. They were particularly interested in the one about his sister.

Kylie led the conversation and told him about their findings and why they had asked to see him.

"We'd love to speak to your sister, Karen if you can tell us where she is." Kylie smiled across the table.

David hunched over his chair. His wrinkles bore deep into his skin. He sipped his drink.

"I have some bad news for you on that count. Karen died three years ago."

"Oh, I am sorry."

"I hope it's not been a wasted journey meeting me."

"No, not at all. Did she speak about her time in the Riverside?" Dotty asked. David wore a cross on a chain around his neck. He clutched hold of it and looked away for a few moments.

"Karen had a secret that she never told me about until she was in her seventies. My first great-grandchild had just been born. It was the first boy. All my other children and grandchildren had been girls. I told Karen about the birth expecting her to be joyful, but she broke down crying. She recounted the horrific things that happened to her." The girls were all ears. David's voice trembled as he recalled the conversation with his sister.

"I was two years younger than Karen, so all I remember was her going away. Our parents told me she had gone away to work. I didn't see her again for over thirty years." David's eyes puffed up, and he wiped a tear from the corner.

"The secret she kept for all those years was that she was raped by her teacher. Because our family were Roman Catholic and didn't agree with abortion, they sent Karen away to have the baby. They didn't want any shame centred around our family. The plan was to have the baby adopted but sadly the child died a few days after Karen gave birth. The baby caught whooping cough and didn't survive."

"Did Karen say where the baby was buried?"

"Here's the thing. She told me she didn't want her baby buried in a mass grave with the others. She wanted her son to be somewhere where she could be close to him and remember him."

"Do you think it could be Karen's baby buried in our friend's grandparent's home?"

"It's possible. I read about a baby's body being found, but I didn't put two and two together. I should probably tell the police what I know, shouldn't I?"

"That would be wise, yes." Dotty demeanour looked sad. "David?" she touched his arm.

"Yes?" He looked over at the girls. His eyes were red. It had taken all his effort to keep it together.

"We are so sorry for what happened to your sister and thank you for sharing what must have been difficult to tell us."

Chapter 20

Dotty and Kylie had such a tale to tell Rachel when they met up on Saturday. Ever since they had spoken to David, something was eating away at Dotty.

"What's wrong, Dotty?" Kylie asked. She could see her friend wasn't her usual chirpy self.

"First thing is, I'm fed up of resisting temptation. I will have a slice of that delicious looking chocolate cake sat in the display cabinet crying out to be eaten."

"Good for you." Kylie was glad that someone was joining her indulging in something naughty. Rachel rarely did because she didn't have a sweet tooth and had the figure to vouch for that.

"You said first thing, is there anything else?"

"Very observant of you, Kylie. We'll make a detective of you, yet." Dotty wagged a finger at her friend and smiled.

"What's concerning me is what David said about the Riverside."

"What was that then?" Rachel asked as she took a sip of her raspberry leaf tea and put her China cup back on the saucer.

"He said that Karen told him she didn't want her baby being buried with the others. Is there a cemetery in the grounds?"

"I'm not sure. Do you think that's what she meant?"

"Maybe we should go back and check," Kylie said.

"I've been once. They wouldn't take kindly to me snooping around again. You two could go though. They haven't met you before," Dotty said.

"That's a good idea. I could go, saying I'm looking at their services as a potential place for my grandad."

Rachel laughed. "Grandad would kill me if he thought I was trying to put him in a home.

"Yes, if you two have a thorough look. See if there are any signs of a cemetery. Two pairs of eyes are better than one."

Rachel and Kylie went over to the care home on Tuesday after Rachel finished work. The residents had just eaten their evening meal. The manager showed them around.

"I'm particularly interested in the gardens. My grandad is a keen gardener, Rachel lied. "He needs somewhere where he can plant some things.

"Do you have a cemetery here?" Kylie asked. The manager pulled a face at Kylie as if to say — what are you on? Kylie noticed the strange expression and quantified her question.

"It's just that Rachel's grandad has a very old dog. It won't live much longer, so if there is somewhere that George could bury Misty then that would swing it for him wanting to live here.

"I see," said the woman who obviously didn't see. In fact, she had never heard such a strange request.

"No, there's no cemetery here," she frowned.

"Any area that is good for growing stuff?" Kylie smiled but was met with a frown.

"There is an area behind the kitchens that the gardener uses as a compost patch. Apparently, it's good for growing vegetables." Kylie smiled and nodded.

As soon as the girls got outside the building they broke down in fits of giggles.

"How did you come up with such a far-fetched story and who is Misty for goodness sake?" Rachel laughed.

"It was the first name that rolled off my tongue. I'd just heard the song Misty Blue on the radio. Did you see the look the manager gave me? She thought I was off my trolley."

"She's not far wrong." Rachel laughed.

When the girls relayed their findings back to Dotty, her reply wasn't what they expected.

"There's only one thing for it."

"What's that, Dotty?"

"We need to go digging?"

"What, you mean literally?"

"That's right. I've got my suspicions that their compost heap may contain a few surprises."

"No, surely not."

"There's one way to find out."

They decided that if they were to dig, the best time to do it would be when it was dark and after it rained. The ground would be easier to churn up. Therefore, their plan was reliant on the weather. From what the girls had discovered, the only security for the building was inside the home and the grounds weren't secure. They knew there was CCTV near the entrance but hadn't spotted any other cameras. They did their reccy and got their tools in place. It was a waiting game. They had to hold fire and wait for the weather to come up trumps.

On Monday night they got what they were looking for. It had been raining cats and dogs all day and still hadn't eased off. Dotty set her alarm for 3 am. The other girls did likewise. Dotty got dressed in her black turtle-neck jumper and black jeans. Her darkest coat was a navy blue one which wasn't waterproof. In the end, she settled for her yellow rain mac with matching sou'wester hat and wellies. She sent a quick text to the other two.

Mission on. Meet at the gates of our target location at 03.30. Don't forget your spade. Check no one is following you. Destroy this message on impact.

It might have sounded over the top, but she loved the idea of being a spy and working incognito. The rain was still pelting down when she crept out of her house and hurried along the road. There were no cars about. She looked suspicious walking along carrying a spade in the middle of the night. They had decided that if they got caught, they would come clean and tell the truth. The only reason they had not gone to the police about their hunch was because it sounded a bit random and the police might not take them seriously. They doubted they would find anything but wanted to be sure.

Rachel and Kylie had a go at Dotty's attire when they saw her.

"You stick out like a sore thumb wearing yellow. I thought we were wearing camouflage?"

"Yes, but it's raining, and I don't want to get wet. You've no room to talk, Rachel. You look like the Pink Panther in that get-up." Rachel wore a grey raincoat with the collar turned up. She had borrowed her dad's trilby hat to keep her hair dry. Kylie was the only one who dressed the part. She had a dark bobble hat on with a dark blue rain jacket and dark waterproof pants. She had even camouflaged her spade in a black bin liner, so it didn't look too obvious walking down the street.

The three girls scurried up the drive. Thankfully, no cars had driven past on their way to the care home. They avoided the camera by the entrance. They rushed down the path at the side of the building towards the kitchen area. There were security lights dotted around. Luckily, the one at the side of the building didn't come on. The light at the back made them jump when it flashed. If the night staff saw any brightness, the girls hoped they would think it was a fox or other animal poking around. The rain had soaked the ground as good as the rum did in Dotty's homemade Christmas cake. The trio squelched up the path towards the compost area.

"We should start digging here," Rachel whispered, pointing to the spot. None of the three looked forward to this dirty work, but it was necessary and as the first spade hit the mud, water ran and collected in the space left. Dotty pulled a face. She didn't like mud at the best of times. Even a mud face pack made her squeamish. She prayed that she wouldn't see any worms and have to scream out. That would certainly blow their cover.

Silently, the girls dug and continued to dig. It was a thankless task. Dotty was the hero of the hour because she had thought to bring a flask of coffee. They stopped to take a breather. Rachel felt weary. She wondered how she would last all day at work without falling asleep. It was 4:40 a.m. and they had been digging for over an hour when Kylie spotted something.

"Guys, is that a bone?" Rachel took out her phone and pressed down for the torch. Dotty shone her dad's large torch on the scene. They could hardly contain their excitement. With muddy hands, Kylie picked up the piece and tried to wipe it clean. It was definitely a bone.

At that moment they realised they hadn't thought their escapade through. How were they going to explain any discovery to the authorities? It was too late for that.

Suddenly the kitchen lights came on and the back of the building lit up like a Christmas tree.

"Who's there?" a voice cried.

Chapter 21

"What are you doing trespassing in our grounds?" the large black care worker asked. Her bulky frame had somehow been squeezed into a uniform two sized too small and the buttons by her bust looked like they would pop open any minute. A security guard joined her. Three more care workers arrived, and the girls were escorted inside. Things looked no better when the police arrived.

"Well, well well, what have we here?" The police officer seemed amused rather than disturbed by the sight in front of him. He held onto his lapel and rocked back and forth on his size ten boots. His older colleague looked more serious, with his arms folded.

The friends may have been better saying they were going to a fancy-dress party with their strange attire. Dotty looked like she was dressed as Paddington bear, Rachel resembled Inspector Clouseau and Kylie looked for all the world like a cat burglar. It was a good job she wasn't there on her own as the crowd may have been more suspicious, especially as now she also had a muddy face. It was hard to take them seriously and when they all started talking at once, the police officer had to intervene.

"Enough," he said in a voice loud enough to wake the entire care home. He put the palm of his hand out to stamp his authority. "One at a time," he spoke softly.

Dotty was the spokesperson and ran through the sequence of events as best she could with Kylie and Rachel chirping in when they felt extra information was needed. Their rendition of what happened took forty minutes, with everyone butting in to ask questions.

Somehow, Rachel didn't think she would make it into work today.

Sergeant Lockyear could have been led astray by the rants of the care home staff. They wanted the girls locking up for trespassing. Thankfully, his police training had taught him not to be swayed by comments from the public. He remembered the exact words of his tutor at police college — use your noggin. Sergeant Lockyear believed he had more than a degree of common sense. He could weight scenes up quickly. This situation was unusual. Nothing like it ever came up in his training, but he thought he was a good judge of character. When he decided what to do in these circumstances, there was one undeniable piece of evidence staring him in the face — the bone now lying on the kitchen table.

As everyone finished putting their two penneth in, he looked at his colleague. They nodded together and looked at the bone. There was that moment in a police officer's life where if you intuitively did the right thing, it could mean promotion or at least a bonus for getting it right. Sergeant Lockyear suspected this was one of those moments. He radioed for back-up.

The three girls were escorted off the premises once they'd shown the officers where they discovered the bone. They were taken to the police station to give statements. The girls were let off with a stern warning.

"Do not to go poking your noses into business that is nothing to do with you again," Sergeant Lockyear said.

Once outside, the girls breathed a sigh of relief.

"That was a lucky escape, we could have been arrested." Rachel hugged her friends.

"What would your dad say, Dotty?" Kylie asked.

"The least my dad knows the better but somehow I don't think I can keep this one from him."

"No, we're likely to be in the news." Rachel looked at her friend's face. It was beaming. "You look very happy with yourself, Dotty?"

"Did you see how long Sergeant Lockyear's eyelashes were?" The other two looked at each other. "And those dark, dreamy eyes had a twinkle in them as soon as he saw us." Kylie and Rachel sniggered. "Don't you think Sergeant Lockyear is rather dishy?"

"So that's it. He probably let us off because he saw you giving him one of your looks."

"What do you mean?"

"Your strike-a-pose face, where you pout. You know the one." Rachel pouted, and the friends laughed.

"Come on, let's get you lot home," Kylie said.

Excavation work started at the home. The bone that Kylie unearthed was found to be human remains. After finding three right legs, the police realised they were in for a long night. Twenty-two other bodies of babies or children were dug up in the grounds of the building. Cataloguing this find was not an overnight job. It could take an eternity to uncover the truth.

What came out of their inquiries was more shocking than anyone imagined. The police interviewed elderly women who had been sent away from their homes once they got pregnant. They were banished from respectable society never to return to their families. Some remains were stillborn babies, but others were toddlers.

The police painstakingly went through the records they found. They were put in touch with a journalist, Ann Passmore who had started to suspect that the running of the home hadn't always been above board. Records showed that some of the children who were born were emaciated. None of the deaths had been recorded on the national death register.

The age of the bodies found ranged from infancy to seven years old. There was much research to carry out. One thing was clear, the children had not been buried according to the rites of the Catholic church. They were not in a consecrated official graveyard.

Dotty suspected that Father Tom knew more than he was letting on, but when interviewed he denied knowing anything about what went on at the home. The other Catholic nuns and priests continued their wall of silence, but there was a public outcry about the findings. Ann Passmore came to interview the three friends to get quotes from them. They described how shocking the discoveries were. Most people involved would be dead or elderly, so the police had to decide if taking any action would be worthwhile.

Chapter 22

Dotty, Rachel and Kylie had opened a can of worms. The investigations could go on for years. Whether anyone would get to the truth, who knew? There would be speculation and theories as to how the babies ended up buried in the grounds. Foul play was ruled out, but the children hadn't had a proper burial. That would now be arranged in every case.

The three girls got their picture in the paper. The trouble was the journalist wanted them to wear the attire they wore that fateful night they made their discovery in the care home grounds. They weren't too pleased. Only Kylie was keen to go ahead. In the end, she talked the other two around. Dotty wore her yellow sou'wester coat, hat and wellies. Rachel was in her grey raincoat with fetching trilby and Kylie looked dark and moody. They took centre stage on the front page of the local rag.

Their short-lived fame didn't go to their heads though. They still went along each Saturday to the local tea rooms. No one asked for their autographs, but Dotty's business grew. The pub where Kylie worked got busier. Punters came for a nosey at the woman who found the first body. Rachel had a string of suitors at her door. At last, she could pie Marvin off.

During their investigations, the police also discovered that the remains in George's garden were Karen Southgate's baby. Arrangements were made for her son to have a proper burial. All the girls attended the funeral along with many of the local people. David Southgate couldn't thank them enough for persevering with their research. Dotty fought back the tears as the baby's body was lowered into the ground at the local cemetery. Her sadness wasn't just for Karen Southgate but for all the unmarried mothers who had lost their children. As she stood up to leave, she noticed many of her neighbours were walking away. There was one couple who she would rather not have bumped into — Hans and Molly. Since that day when she was found in the bush in their garden, she had avoided them. She couldn't avoid them this time as they headed right towards her. She still hadn't made amends to them for her outburst and accusations.

"I'm sorry for accusing you of having an affair."

"Don't worry about it. It's water under the bridge now." Hans said.

"How are rehearsals for the show going?"

"Very well, our first performance is next week."

Even Hans mellowed towards Dotty. His smile brimmed from ear to ear when she turned up on his doorstep at weekend with a coffee and walnut cake that she had made especially for them. A dickie bird in the shape of her mum had told her it was their seventeenth wedding anniversary.

"I'm sure it's walnuts for seventeen," she said as she passed over the tin containing the cake. Molly looked confused. "You know, like silver for twenty-five. Actually, I've just made that up."

"Why, thank you, Dotty. You're most kind. Hey, if you hang on a minute, Hans has something for you." Dotty stood in the doorway waiting.

"Here's a present for you and your friends." Dotty didn't like to open the envelope he passed her there and then, so she waited until she got home. She looked inside. It was three tickets for *A Steamy Romance* starring Hans and Greta.

The three girls sat there the following week chomping away at their popcorn. They watched Hans cracking his whip and chuckled. Greta's performance as a lady of the night was brilliant. Dotty was pleased they dimmed the lights because her cheeks glowed pink as she thought back to what she suspected. She didn't always get things right, but she was glad she followed her hunches. Hans and Molly had forgiven her because they had a strong solid marriage. She was happy that she acted on her hunch over Karen's baby. She may have dished the dirt on Hans and got it wrong but dishing the dirt on the Riverside had revealed a lot. No arrests were made from what was uncovered. The incidents happened too long ago. The positive outcome was that at least the children who died now had a proper burial.

There was another outcome that went through Dotty's mind. She had been introduced to a handsome young policeman in the shape of Sergeant Lockyear. He had left an impression on her with the masterful way he handled the situation at the care home. She sat there daydreaming about what the future may hold and smiled.

Dotty Dishes the Dirt is a novella and prequel to the Dotty Drinkwater Mystery series.
I hope you enjoyed it.

Book 1 will be coming out soon. If you want to know when, you can sign up to my VIP club

I am looking to build a relationship up with my readers, so I send out occasional newsletters to people who join my VIP club. These include otherwise untold information about the characters, things about me, and other bits of news including freebies and offers.

I would love you to join and in return for giving me your email which will never be passed on to third parties, you will receive exciting goodies and give-aways not found anywhere else.

You can find the sign-up page on my website at:

http://dezzardwriter.com/mc4wp-form-preview

Website: http://dezzardwriter.com/
Email: support@dezzardwriter.com
Facebook: https://www.facebook.com/dezzardwriter/
Twitter: https://twitter.com/diane_ezzard

REVIEWS

If you enjoyed this book, I would greatly appreciate if you would leave a review.
Just a few short words on Amazon and maybe Goodreads and Bookbub would go a long way towards helping me.
Your encouragement helps stoke the fires of my creativity.

To improve my writing and to spur me on to write more, it is important that I get feedback from you, my readers.
Your opinion matters to me.
I greatly appreciate your time and effort.

You can leave your review here - mybook.to/dottypre

ABOUT THE AUTHOR

Manchester born Diane Ezzard writes emotionally charged mystery books about ordinary people dealing with everyday situations until something goes badly wrong. (There is usually a dead body in there somewhere).

Her first series - the Sophie Brown Mystery Series is dark and gritty. The second series - the Dotty Drinkwater Mystery Series is a cozy, full of zany lighthearted escapades.

In a previous life, she worked as a HR manager, counsellor and managed a charity among many other jobs where she has picked up a lot of her material from. She now lives and works in South-East England close to her daughter and young grandchildren where she spends her time fighting pirates and dinosaurs when not writing.

ACKNOWLEDEMENTS

A big thank you goes to Samantha Ezzard for the great looking cover.
Thanks go especially to my team of readers and my fan base.
Without your praise and encouragement, I would not be spurred on to continue writing the way that I am.

LINKS: -

    Website: http://dezzardwriter.com/
    Email: support@dezzardwriter.com
    Facebook: https://www.facebook.com/dezzardwriter/
    Twitter: https://twitter.com/diane_ezzard
    Bookbub: http://bit.ly/2OlnLE1
    Amazon: https://amzn.to/2Qf2uZV

Dotty Dices with Death

Book 1 in the Dotty Drinkwater Mystery Series.

"Suspicious death of local DJ," read the headlines. The man of Dotty's dreams turns into something of a nightmare.

Meeting the tall, dark, handsome foreigner at her new job in the casino, Dotty thought all her Christmases had come at once. Instead, she discovers a trail of lies and deceit, to say nothing of a suspicious package.

Was Dotty the last one to see him alive? Do the police suspect she is involved?

With the help of her friends, Dotty sets out to unravel the mystery around the tragic murder before she gets locked up herself.

She should never have ignored the warning given by the mystery woman.

Available through Amazon - mybook.to/dotdice

Chapter 1

Dotty took off her fluffy olive-green beanie hat and scratched the top of her head. She made her way to the back of the bus and found an empty seat by the window. As CEO of her own company, it wasn't ideal travelling this way. It couldn't be helped, however, as her car had been making that funny noise again. She wouldn't put up with it any longer. After all, it might be something serious and she could hardly run her gardening business with no vehicle. So, she dropped it off at the garage first thing. It was handy that she had no customers booked in today other than a potential new client to visit. She'd look strange getting on the bus with a lawnmower and other gardening tools. What would her nosey neighbour, Betty Simpson think? There would be no end of moaning from Betty if she took up extra room with her equipment. Nudging Betty who sat on the seat in front, she smiled.

"Cold out, today," she said.

"Yes, dear. Where's your car?" Betty didn't miss a trick. She was the go-to person if you wanted to hear any gossip.

"It's in the garage for a service." That wasn't the whole truth but sometimes a little white lie was the easiest option with Betty. Dotty was in no mood for explaining irregular car noises this morning. Betty didn't need to know the ins and outs. She embroidered stories enough and came up with her own version, anyway. Knowing Betty, if she decided that Dotty's car had really been towed away for getting behind with the repayments, then that's what she would tell everyone.

Betty could tarnish your name with her misrepresentations before you could click your fingers.

Dotty thought about changing her car for a van. It would be more practical, but it didn't go with her image and street cred. Besides, she was fed up of gardening. It was okay in the summer months when the weather was warmer but now the colder weather had set in, there wasn't as much to do, and it was freezing working outside. She'd not given that much thought when she was talked into starting up this little one-woman business by her two friends, Rachel and Kylie.

It was alright for them. They both had their nice warm jobs working inside. Rachel worked in an office and Kylie worked as a barmaid at Ye Olde Six Bells. Neither girl was happy in their jobs, but they weren't as miserable as Dotty. They always had a moan when the threesome met up on a Saturday. Although, if they all wanted to go on holiday together next year, they would have to grin and bear it.

Dotty wasn't on the bus for long. She checked the address beforehand and knew which stop to get off. If the Braithwaite's hadn't lived at the top of a hill, she'd have taken her pushbike, but it was too steep to tackle, and the forecast was for rain later. She shuddered and vowed to put some effort into looking for a new job. There had to be better ways than this to make a living. It could be worse. She could be in India working in the paddy fields or — no she couldn't think of any jobs worse than gardening right now. Even India would be warmer than Sussex. She looked out the window and watched a gust of wind pick up the leaves as they took flight through the air.

Dotty arrived at the location and jumped off the bus. She immediately felt the chill of the wind on her cheeks. She tossed her head back and walked up to the house. Her mind wandered as she thought about working in a bar in Ibiza or picking strawberries in Portugal, anything warm away from this biting cold weather. She looked up at the large house and groaned as she rang the doorbell. The door creaked open and the tall, pinched face of Mr Braithwaite stared down at her as she stood waiting on the bottom step.

"Oh, you're a girl. Well, I suppose its women's lib, and anything goes these days. You'd better come through." He walked in front and Dotty scurried behind. "It's a girl, Marjorie. It's a girl." Dotty thought it sounded like someone had just given birth.

"Yes, I know it is, Albert. Now run along and make yourself useful." Albert stood in the doorway frowning. "Make a drink." She shooed him out of the room. "Have a seat. Dotty, isn't it?"

Dotty nodded and plonked herself down on a grey corduroy sofa. The Braithwaite couple were retired, and Mrs Braithwaite had seen Dotty's card in the local hairdresser's shop. Albert returned not long after with a tray of drinks and a plate of chocolate digestives. Under normal circumstances, Dotty would refuse the biscuits as she was dieting again, but she took one to be polite.

"Take a few. We only get them in for guests. We both have diabetes and can't eat them." Dotty thought it strange to buy biscuits they couldn't eat, so she took another two to show her consideration and smiled. She finished her drink and Marjorie asked her all the questions she could think of. Marjorie wanted to know more about Dotty's family than finding out her prowess as a gardener. In fact, the only question relating to gardening was about her age.

"You look very young to have your own gardening business, dear."

"I'm twenty-seven."

"Gosh, you don't look that old." Dotty believed her youthful looks were more down to her beauty regime than her genes. She used a face pack twice a week, exfoliated on alternate days, always used serum and moisturiser and gave her face a deep cleanse every bedtime. She had also recently splashed out on eye cream and neck cream because you can't be too careful. Wrinkles could appear any time. With all the effort she put in, she hoped to still look youthful in her sixties and seventies if she could keep up her efforts until then.

"Thank you," Dotty said, blushing.

"So, you're not married, yet?" Marjorie asked as she pointed to Dotty's bare wedding ring finger.

"No, I'm very much single. My last relationship was a disaster. Ray was a nightmare to get rid of. He just wouldn't take no for an answer. We were only together for a short time and it's taken me months to get him to see I'm not interested."

"Oh dear, young love never runs smooth. Those were the days. I knew straightaway when I met my Albert that he was the one for me. You know immediately, don't you, dear?"

"I wish Ray could have worked out sooner he wasn't the one for me. He must have been thick not to get the message." Marjorie gave a shallow sigh. From her nostalgic gaze, she was no longer listening to Dotty. Her memory cells sprang forward with visions of Albert as a young man with his long hair. They were both teenagers in the Swinging Sixties but were more mod than rocker. Albert owned a gleaming blue scooter and would take Marjorie on day trips to Southend. Ah, those were the days.

"Would you like me to show you the work we want you to do?" Marjorie asked, coming back into the moment.

"Yes, of course."

"Follow me. There's a lot." Marjorie pulled a face. "Albert can't do it anymore with his bad back."

They walked around to the back of the house. Dotty was taken out to the garden.

"Wow, that's huge."

"Yes, it's rather deceptive. You can't tell from the front of the house just how much land is round the back. As you can see, we have a lot of trees which means a lot of leaves." Dotty had never seen as many leaves as those sat in the Braithwaite's' garden. It was as though they had been collecting them up for her. "Do you have one of those machines that hoover them up?"

"No, but I'm sure I can get hold of one." She stood admiring the hues of orange and brown that nature produced in autumn just before the harshness of winter took the last few leaves away. There were speckles of yellow and red to inspire her creative juices. As Dotty spoke, a gust of wind brought another ton of leaves swirling into the garden. She worried that as soon as one set of leaves cleared, another would appear. She'd have preferred to be out there painting the scenery rather than clearing it away.

The two women stood together viewing the spectacle for some time. More leaves fell from the interlocking branches of the trees above. This would be a thankless task. It wasn't a good idea to take this job on, but Dotty needed the money. She was at the stage of borrowing off her mum to go on a night out and that wasn't good.

They moved into the kitchen to discuss terms. Dotty didn't know how much hiring a leaf machine would set her back, so she added on extra to compensate. She showed Marjorie the price as she seemed to be in charge and the one holding the purse strings in this house. They had just shaken on the deal when a crashing sound came from the hall. Both women looked at each other with raised eyebrows.

"It's only me, Gran," came a voice that Dotty thought she recognised. She frowned and seconds later a tall young man stood at the kitchen door.

"Oh, it's you. What are you doing here?" he swept his lanky fringe off to the side.

"Hello, Ray. How are you?" Dotty had a sickly feeling growing inside her stomach.

"Do you two know each other?" Marjorie looked at them both.

Book One in the Sophie Brown series –

I KNOW YOUR EVERY MOVE

A sinister phone call, an unknown visitor. Sophie's life is about to be turned upside down

Sophie has worked hard to free herself from the clutches of addiction and turn her life around. Practising as a counsellor, in a women's centre in Manchester, she now helps other girls in trouble.

She forms a close relationship with Cassie, one of her clients and tries to help her escape the clutches of a violent boyfriend.

But is Sophie being followed?

How can she uncover the truth, when she can't trust what is real?
The more she delves, the closer she gets to danger.
Can she revisit her own dark past before it is too late?

Get hooked on this dark, twist-filled suspense thriller that's in the vein of works by Rachel Abbott and Mark Edwards.

Available through Amazon - mybook.to/ikyem

Chapter One

YESTERDAY

Something soft and feathery brushed past the end of my nose. I sneezed and opened my eyes.

"Oh Max," I said.

The vision of loveliness that met me made me smile. What an adorable furry sight to wake up to in the morning. Sat on top of the silver satin duvet cover lay Max, the new addition to my family. At twelve-weeks-old, Max was a cute, mischievous bundle of joy. With big doleful eyes looking up at me, my heart melted. I stroked his velvety golden coat and tickled him under his chin.

"Want your breakfast, Max?"

I ignored the sound of him purring as I pressed my phone and looked at the time. 6.42. I groaned. I didn't need to get up early today. It was Saturday, so no work and I'd had a fitful night's sleep.

I'd had that dream again. The same one I'd been having over the last few months. I was running away from something or someone. I didn't know what, but I always woke up full of tension and fear. Thankfully, I never got caught. One minute I was jogging by the river, on my usual route, the next I'd been transported to a house. The combination of the red poppy wallpaper and mint green leather sofa was a scene I knew well from my childhood. Mum stood by the mirror in the hall, carefully putting on her lipstick. She wore the last outfit I'd seen her in, a tan polo neck ribbed jumper and fawn herringbone tweed skirt. I pulled at her arm.

"Please come, Mum." She didn't acknowledge me.
"Mum, come on, we need to go." No response.
"Hurry up Mum." Still, she ignored me.

I wasn't happy. Whether it was the bright shade of her crimson lip colour I didn't like or the fact she didn't respond to me, I didn't know.

In the dream, I began to panic as I sensed trouble brewing. I kept looking around. I had to act now. I tried one last time, shaking her.

"Mum, Mum, we've got to leave." She continued to face the mirror.

"Come on Mum, we've got to go."

I shouted out, but Mum still didn't acknowledge me. I began to cry. Fear enveloped me. I knew we were in danger. I watched her as she slowly applied another coat of lipstick and massaged her lips against each other. She didn't respond to me, so I turned away from her and ran.

That was when I woke up. Slowly, I re-entered the land of the living with a big stretch. Max jumped off the bed. My palms were sweating, and my pulse was racing. The anxiety rose in my chest. I had left Mum again and even though I knew it was only a dream, I didn't feel good. My stomach ached as I thought of the memories of her.

Might as well get up now I'm awake, I thought and walked over to open the curtains. I squinted as I looked outside. It wasn't the brightness of the day that greeted me. The clouds looked grey and forlorn. I begrudgingly put my dressing gown on and pottered into the kitchen.

I had Max now to look after, and I enjoyed spoiling him. My first job in a morning was to get him a saucer of milk and his food.

"Come on Max, here's your breakfast," I said. He didn't even give me the chance to get the food out of the can. He had his nose busy poking inside, trying to get at the fishy delights.

There weren't many places for a kitten to wander around and explore, especially with a flat as small as mine. When he got bigger, I knew I would have to let him out to discover the big wide world, and that scared me.

After feeding Max, I reached up into the cupboard to get the breakfast cereal. I sat for a few minutes, crunching a mouthful of fruit and fibre, contemplating the day ahead. Saturday usually meant doing chores which I detested, followed by a trip down to the shops to get my groceries for the weekend.

Shopping list done, I began milling around the place, starting with tidying up the kitchen. After walking into the hall to get the mop out of the cupboard, I checked myself out in the mirror.

My hair looked tangled, so I picked up the hairbrush and brushed it. It had a sheen and style that many women envied. I loved the comments I got about my beautiful long red locks.

The flat never seemed lonely on a Saturday, thanks to James Martin. Saturday Morning Kitchen was a favourite TV programme of mine. It formed part of my weekend ritual that included eating a bacon butty for lunch and a curry later that night. I didn't think of myself as a creature of habit, but there were certain behaviours that ran so deep, they were a regular part of my life now.

I had a passion for food, which spanned from cooking to watching cookery programmes on TV. I owned a vast range of recipe books and of course, I loved eating. Thankfully, I enjoyed running, as my frame would have been a lot larger had I not.

I wasn't one to try new recipes; I usually kept to classics like chilli and fish pie. I often dreamed of being the head chef of a Michelin-starred restaurant. Sadly, the culinary skills I possessed fell a long way short of that. Sometimes, I'd be in the shower, merrily singing away and realise that the sound accompanying me wasn't violins but the smoke detector going off in the other room. I would then remember that I'd put a couple of rashers of bacon under the grill.

I was concentrating on watching Rick Stein making a fish stew before getting up to tackle the ironing. Wrestling to put the ironing board up wasn't easy in the small confines of the kitchen. There was very little room to manoeuvre. I sighed heavily and frowned. I didn't like housework, least of all the ironing.

Suddenly the house phone rang. The old-fashioned cream coloured telephone sat a few feet from where I stood. I'd bought it to tone in with my muted decor. The penetrating sound of the intermittent bell ringing made me jump, and with jerked shoulders, I listened intently to the shrill tone. It was unusual to hear the house phone these days. Most people phoned me on my mobile. In fact, I only used the landline for the internet, so I couldn't imagine who it could be. Only Dad rang me on the landline, and we had a set time every Sunday night to speak. He never detracted from that, so I knew it couldn't be him. I decided not to answer. It was probably one of those PPI compensation calls or the ones that ask if you've been involved in an accident.

The phone got louder with every ring. The noise had distracted me from the ironing, and lacking concentration, I hadn't realised that I'd misjudged the iron plate. The hot iron toppled over, and I instinctively put my hand out to catch it.

Damn, I swore under my breath. The heat of the iron burnt through to my fingers and I screamed out. I was annoyed with myself for being so stupid. I quickly managed to shimmy past the ironing board to get to the sink. I put my hand under the cold-water tap. Ow, did that hurt. I kept my fingers under the icy blast of water, and I heard the phone still ringing.

That didn't sound like a friendly bell, more like the harsh warning sound of a siren. The loud noise blocked out the pleasant familiar tones of the omelette competition on TV. I urged the phone to stop. My heart pounded, and my fingers throbbed with pain. Why didn't it stop? I became irritated. The constant sound of the phone began to take on a macabre tone, and I became afraid to remove my hand from under the cold flow of water. Should I answer? No, I've left it this long.

My mind started playing tricks on me. Memories flooded back of a time when I had been trapped in the clutches of someone else's obsessions. A shudder came over me. What if it's him? No, I knew I was being silly now.

What if it's important? Pull yourself together, girl. If it's urgent, they'll leave a message, I told myself. I turned the tap off at the same time the phone stopped ringing. I picked up the remote control and turned off the TV.

The silence was eerie, and I could feel the thudding of my pulse. A knot churned over in my stomach and nausea crept up from my guts into my throat. My palms started to sweat, and the perspiration dripped from my forehead. My mouth was dry. A tightness developed in my chest and I bit my lip. Why was I getting so nervous about a phone ringing?

I walked over to the table, tentatively picking up the receiver with my good hand. My nerves erupted when I heard the tone that indicated there had been a message left. Stop getting so worked up, girl.

This was stupid. Breathing rapidly, I took the phone to my ear. A wave of cold air came over me as I listened intently. And I listened, and I listened. Nothing. I breathed a sigh of relief. Probably one of those nuisance companies, I thought.

I shook my throbbing hand and decided to leave the ironing until another time. I went into the bathroom to get a shower. I stood under the hot water for longer than normal and I chastised myself for getting so worked up over the phone. The water poured down, covering my body. The heat of it felt good. My fingers were still smarting. The shower door normally gave adequate sound proofing but, even with soap in my ears, I heard the ringtone of the house phone again.

I'll leave it, I thought to myself. It's probably the same annoying company that rung earlier. The ringing had stopped by the time I got out but, when I reached for the towel, it started up again. I was becoming irritated now.

Briskly drying myself down, I put on my dressing gown then went back into the kitchen to make myself a drink. I put the water in the kettle. The phone started ringing again. Whoever was phoning certainly wasn't taking no for an answer, so I decided to check the phone for messages in case an emergency had come up.

I knew I shouldn't be agitated over this, but I'd had such bad experiences in the past with menacing calls. I now had an unfounded fear around phones. Blind panic overwhelmed me as I listened and heard the distorted robot-like voice of a text call coming through the receiver.

"DON'T THINK YOU CAN GET AWAY WITH THIS."

What on earth did that mean? Get away with what? It was a strange message, and I didn't understand. Then I realised there was another message to listen to, so I pressed the button and waited.

In the same spooky, tinny voice of technology I heard, "SLUTS END UP GETTING WHAT THEY DESERVE." I started shaking.

I wondered if I could have misheard the messages so played them again. No, there was no mistaking the words. I pressed in the digits to find out the number the calls had been sent from, but the voice came back, 'Caller number withheld.'

I walked over to the sofa and sat down, my shoulders hunched, slowly taking in what had just happened. I wrapped my arms around my body and rocked from side to side, thinking. Was this a wrong number and all a mistake or could this be something more sinister?

Bibliography

The Sophie Brown Mystery Series –

My Dark Decline – prequel   mybook.to/mdd

One woman's journey from oblivion to recovery

I Know Your Every Move – Book 1
mybook.to/ikyem

A sinister phone call, an unknown visitor — is Sophie being followed?

As Sick As Our Secrets - Book 2   mybook.to/asaos

Secrets and lies are rife in the dark world of gangsters and criminals.

The Sinister Gathering - Book 3   mybook.to/singat

Sophie went on a retreat hoping to find peace, instead, she found the body of a woman she had just met

Resentments and Revenge – Book 4
mybook.to/resandrev

A murdered young woman, a missing schoolboy, are they connected?

A Life Lost – Book 5   mybook.to/allost

She lost her memory and then her life.

The Killing Cult – Book 6 mybook.to/tsg

Sophie makes a horrific discovery when she stumbles on a deadly cult.

The Dotty Drinkwater Mystery Series -

Dotty Dishes the Dirt – prequel
mybook.to/dottypre

Dotty unearths more than she bargains for when she digs up human bones.

Dotty Dices with Death – Book 1
mybook.to/dotdice

The man of Dotty's dreams turns into a nightmare when he is found dead under suspicious circumstances.

Printed in Dunstable, United Kingdom